THE ALPHONSE COURRIER AFFAIR

"Fast-paced, gripping and resonant with emotions more usually associated with Greek tragedy"

PATRICIA DUNCKER, *New Statesman*

"A tale of hidden passions and big secrets by this most polished of writers" *Tutto Libri*

"Reminiscent of Francois Mauriac's unsparing dramatisations of passions held in check until they inevitably, catastrophically erupt . . . Morazzoni's best book yet" ***Kirkus Reviews***

"An ingeniously wrought puzzle that amply confirms the narrative gift of this shrewd detective of human passions"

MARIAPIA BONANOTE, *Famiglia Cristiana*

"Superb . . . a tremendously well-crafted novel, perfectly paced and displaying meticulous language and razor wit"

PHILIP HERTER, *St Petersburg Times*

D0281603

MARTA MORAZZONI was born in Milan in 1950. She teaches literature in a secondary school. She has written three novels and a volume of short stories, *Girl in a Turban*, described by *The Times* as "subtle, ironic, an altogether outstanding collection of stories". *The Alphonse Courrier Affair* was the winner of the prestigious Campiello Prize and the *Independent* Foreign Fiction Award, which is awarded to the author and translator jointly.

EMMA ROSE won the John Florio prize with the first book she translated, Marta Morazzoni's novel *His Mother's House*.

Marta Morazzoni

THE ALPHONSE COURRIER AFFAIR

Translated from the Italian by
Emma Rose

THE HARVILL PRESS
LONDON

First published in Italian with the title *Il Caso Courrier* by Longanesi & C., Milan, 1997

First published in Great Britain in 2000 by The Harvill Press

This paperback edition first published in 2001 by
The Harvill Press, 2 Aztec Row, Berners Road, London N1 0PW

www.harvill.com

1 3 5 7 9 8 6 4 2

© Longanesi & C., 1997
English translation © Emma Rose, 1999, 2000

Marta Morazzoni asserts the moral right to be identified as the author of this work

A CIP catalogue record for this book is available from the British Library

ISBN 1 86046 944 2

Typeset in Garamond at Libanus Press, Marlborough, Wiltshire

Printed and bound in Great Britain by Mackays of Chatham

To Maud, Luciano and all of us,
conspirators of an autumn evening

THE ALPHONSE
COURRIER AFFAIR

PROLOGUE

In the year 1917 the Courrier affair erupted quite without warning into the consciousness of a village in the Auvergne. The village itself was not in any way remarkable; it possessed nothing of note, except a beautiful Romanesque church – which, by the way, it still possesses, so if any of you happened to be travelling around those parts, ideally in summer, since in winter it can snow very heavily and make it far from easy . . . But all this has nothing to do with the affair which blew up in 1917, although, now I come to think of it, that also occurred in winter, just after one of those heavy snowfalls. The church, incidentally, looks most impressive against the snow, so dark and powerful in the small, white-clad square. It would be worth making the effort, in spite of the difficulties . . .

Anyway, it was the penultimate year of the war, and a very hard year, in terms both of the weather and the nation's waning strength. Although for this village in the Auvergne, where the Courrier affair exploded like a grenade, the importance of the war was only relative. These things always seem more terrible in retrospect than in reality – than in some people's realities, at any rate.

At the time of the affair – which, upon reflection, in Paris would never have been considered an "affair" at all, just a routine matter: how true it is that what counts is when and where things happen, rather than how. A village, as they say down in the Auvergne, is a place which, by its very nature, requires a certain amount of news to erupt, like pimples on

3

the skin, and eventually burst. Which explains why, in that year of 1917, second-to-last of the war, this affair acquired such significance.

At the time, as I was saying, Alphonse Courrier ran his own ironmonger's shop. A shop which, on its own, was worth the whole of the rest of the village put together. A dark, impressive shop, lined floor to ceiling with wooden shelves and drawers, and encircled by a metal rail – placed three quarters of the way up the wall – against which rested the ladders that ran the length of the room. The two shop-assistants bravely risked life and limb on these death-traps, particularly the elder and less agile of the two men, whose diligence compensated for the disadvantages of age. Rarely did Courrier himself make use of the ladders.

After the shop and the Romanesque church – which, I should mention, houses a charming little statue of the enthroned Virgin, should anyone happen to be passing . . . Together with those two buildings, as I was saying, the third marvel of the village was Alphonse Courrier himself. Third in order of appearance, because the shop stood opposite the church (the church is the first building you notice on reaching the village) and on weekdays he could generally be found behind his counter. Feel free to prioritise these delights as you see fit.

For the whole of 1917 Alphonse Courrier was fifty years old – quite literally, because he was born on the 1st of January. He was a handsome man: not tall, but well proportioned; strong without being thick-set, and displaying a degree of refinement you might not expect to find in a village. The best of him was in his face: regular features, eyes of a piercing blue – not the insipid blue that so often accompanies light blond hair – which twinkled behind gold-rimmed spectacles, and the gold of a short, well-groomed beard, perhaps cultivated in order to disguise a slightly uneven chin. His hair, in places, showed signs of deserting him, and was in any case too light to be still called blond, but these were details which enhanced, rather than tarnished, the pleasing effect of the whole.

To enter the shop opposite the church was to stray into a dark cave, whose only illumination, in those days, was the warm golden glow of Alphonse Courrier's face.

He was peerless at his trade. Not even the most expert Parisian ironmonger could have equalled him. His skill consisted in giving the impression that he cared nothing for sales and still less for money, which he would place almost absentmindedly in the till. He never counted it in front of his customers, but you could see that he enjoyed his work and that his satisfaction lay in being able to provide anything you could possibly ask for. He had conceived of the business many years before, when nothing of the sort existed in the village, and the locals didn't even believe it was needed.

To return for a moment to that golden glow I described earlier, which lit the gloomy depths of the cave: the glow of Alphonse Courrier's face. I forgot to mention that the effect was enhanced by the burning red end of a cigar, something he was never without. He kept one between his lips more for companionship than out of real addiction, and the habit suited him. Now let us abandon this digression, which was necessary to capture a detail. What, in the life of a village, could be more vital than a detail?

So, the villagers had thought there wasn't any need for an ironmonger's until – in the year 1900 – Courrier opened one for them. It then became self-evident that village history should divide into "before" and "after" the arrival of Courrier's shop; into the days when "you used to have to traipse over the hill to find a decent sickle" and nowadays, when "you can send the boy over to get one, then call in to pay for it later, when you have the time". All the difference in the world! Alphonse

Courrier had not simply been right; more importantly, he'd been farsighted. That was one of his strong points.

Embarking on the chapter of his life headed "Shop" had been relatively straightforward. It just so happened that he was thirty-three, and had some capital, as well as the necessary initiative. He bought the premises from the baker, who was going bankrupt. It was a common enough occurrence for a village baker to go out of business and an ironmonger to step in instead. There was courage, or recklessness, in all this. The usual compromise is to state, with the judgment of Solomon, that both qualities were at play, but in this case it would be untrue: Alphonse Courrier was a very clear thinker, and his had been the courage of calculation. If only men were always so calculating, instead of naively generous, or apparently so.

He was a cultured man – by village standards of course – so he opened his shop on the 21st of March, the first day of spring, because spring is the season for new beginnings. The poet Dante says as much, in one of the passages which is read even in French provincial schools. He calls it "the sweet season" and, as a child, Courrier had stored this information away in his memory for a time when he too would have to begin something important.

When Alphonse Courrier stood in the doorway of his own shop for the first time, he was a less handsome figure than the man he was to become in 1917. Gold requires a patina: the veil of time, which dims the glitter and makes it less . . . less vulgar, one could almost say. In 1900 Alphonse Courrier certainly glittered.

The chapter of his life headed "Marriage" proved more difficult to open.

The problem – if problem it was – lay in the fact that any decision of this kind, far from being the private matter people persist in taking it for, involved the whole village. Let's say

Alphonse Courrier went ahead and chose a woman – and his thirty-year-old good looks would allow him to do just that. Every villager would begin to wonder, and to investigate whether he had made the right choice. When he had given himself to women out of passion, that was, and remained, his own private business, but marriage is quite another matter. For one thing, it has nothing to do with love, as Courrier had realized from the start. Matrimony is a serious affair, while love is totally unreliable. Love does not embrace the concept of duration – a point on which Courrier was adamant: marriage was something to be done once and for all. This conviction of his had nothing to do with churches or sacraments, which he saw merely as ornamental trappings, necessary of course, but only on aesthetic grounds. On the contrary, it was a technical consideration, obvious to anyone with an ounce of good sense. Having a wife meant sharing the same house, the same bed, the same money. Courrier was a long way from being mercenary, everybody knew that, but not far from pragmatism. That was why his bride would need to be approved by the village, which, in his choice, would recognise, commend and admire a man of sound judgment, acumen and taste.

The marriage chapter proved long and slow to initiate; a minefield. But here too he made the right moves, however warily. His lack of haste proved fortuitous, since Fortune, in the long run, favoured him. Bachelorhood was not a burden to him, for obvious reasons, but since he knew it had to end at a certain point, he must, above all, not reach that point unprepared. Even as a child at school, he hated not being ready when it mattered. Making a fool of yourself – now there is something that can ruin your life. Like the time when he was only just eight years old, and in his second year at primary school. His classroom also housed older children, who were already in their third year, and he was a little in awe of them.

One afternoon – he could probably still remember the date – he was in the middle of a geography test. Pupils had to write down the names of the surrounding villages, from the north through the west, south and east. It was difficult, and Alphonse was concentrating on the eastern section, where there were two villages which bordered with each other along slender strips of land, one of which belonged to his uncle. Few other pupils would know that this particular village extended so far, wedging a finger of land into that narrow space. It was a detail which would have earned Alphonse special commendation, above even the big boys in the third year.

Suddenly, his nose began to run. He tried sniffing, to save time, but the slithery warmth of the mucus refused to retreat entirely. The moisture lodged itself in the little canal beneath his nostrils. He put down his pen, drying it carefully, so as not to leave blots of ink on which he might absentmindedly rest the page, and reached for his handkerchief. There was no handkerchief. For the moment the back of his hand would do, but it would not do for long, and in any case it didn't so much dry up the mucus as spread it about evenly. He sniffed with all his might as he picked his pen up again, but he lacked the required suction power and, if the problem had been serious before, now it was beyond repair. It shattered his concentration. The name of his uncle's village – he couldn't remember if it was spelt with a final "s", and this threatened to ruin everything. The viscid taste of mucus on his upper lip was swamping his brain. Then, as though in a fog, he became aware of having seized a sort of dirty, much-used rag which his neighbour had held out to him on a charitable impulse. He dried his nose so ineffectively that a drop of mucus fell on to the page. There was no time to copy the work out again, and in any case they had only been given one sheet of paper. He looked down: beneath the slimy smear he could just distinguish the name of the other village, the one which everybody – even the little children in the first form – was sure to know.

This episode taught Courrier a lesson about life which he never forgot, and not just in relation to handkerchiefs.

Never again would he be caught unprepared. It would be interesting to survey, one by one, the years which separated the handkerchief incident from the fifty-year-old man he was to become in 1917, to confirm how seldom he let events slip from his grasp. I realize it might be a tedious exercise, but I do believe that, were it possible, it would not be without value. It would at least explain the occurrence which seemed to take the whole village by surprise. But we are coming to that.

We were speaking of Courrier's marriage project, which was progressing slowly and deliberately. His thirty-three years suited him. He did not look a year younger, and this was to his advantage, because he had just that hint of mature virility which, in different ways, fascinates both men and women.

His last love had been very beautiful. No, the girl herself was not beautiful. On the contrary, no other man in the village wanted her, because she was rough and graceless: inherently unsuited, you'd have thought, to love (as indeed she was), but Alphonse, steering clear of sentiment, looked initially for passion. And because, until that moment, nobody had wanted her, not even in jest, the poor creature lavished tremendous quantities of passion and unquestioning devotion upon him. Secretly. That was the wonderful thing: the secrecy. She was so good at dissembling that nobody ever suspected what might be happening between them. She did not betray herself to her women friends, resisting the temptation to boast, although she would have had every justification because, at least twice a week, she held in her arms the handsomest man in the village. A man who, admittedly, didn't look her in the face very often, or talk to her very much, but one who did choose to spend the whole night with her.

Once, in the early days of the shop, her father sent her there to get something for their house or land. Alphonse, biting on his cigar as he smiled the same knowing smile he gave to all his customers, served her with polite detachment, in spite of the fact that the shop was empty and there wasn't a single witness, even out in the square, to see or hear anything. It was almost as if he didn't recognise her in daylight.

The secret endured for around two years. It was a methodical, faithful passion. Not that Alphonse had failed to notice other girls who seemed interesting and not marriageable (the fundamental requirement). But he only considered them in passing, even if some would linger in his mind for longer than others, and with more pleasure. His body thrived on this twice-weekly faithfulness. Also, Adèle's cleverness was such that she had not allowed the relationship to alter her in any way. It is usually said of women that, however ugly they may be, the experience of love will always change them a little: it may mellow their expression, smooth their features or give them a dreamy look. Not in Adèle's case, luckily for both of them. Not in the slightest. She remained the ugliest girl in the village, and probably also the happiest. Enthroned in her ugliness, she feared nothing, least of all the passage of time which, far from diminishing her, increased her confidence. Each new night spent with him was something gained, and over the two years Alphonse had never once missed an appointment. How many wives in the village could say as much?

When the time came, Alphonse went so far as to ask the parish priest to put the wedding off by two days, in order (he didn't mention this to the cleric) not to have to alter his private ritual. Of course both he and she were agreed on the necessity to stop, afterwards. And it was then, in one brief moment of gratitude, that Alphonse thought he might even love her. So it was that, the day before leading his official wife to the altar, he retrospectively consecrated two years of subterfuge.

His official wife. A wife is necessary for all sorts of reasons; Courrier knew them all and had weighed them up, one by one. She did not have to be beautiful, but she did have to be a woman of a certain presence — a more complex and subtle quality. She had to have a strong constitution, in order to stay at his side for the rest of his life. These were not emotional considerations, obviously, since they were being assessed in advance, but purely practical. He was terrified by the thought of being left a widower, of having to begin all over again, of not feeling close enough to the person (it never even occurred to him to think of "the woman") who was to share his old age.

He found her in the neighbouring village. She was called Agnès, and she was perfect.

Strange to say, the chapter headed "Children" did not greatly interest him. It was, if I remember correctly, the third chapter of his life, and perhaps the trickiest — the one he felt least able to evaluate. He trod carefully. He had become very good at treading carefully.

Permit me to take a step backwards, to an episode which, again, is marginal but whose inclusion is, I believe, justified: Alphonse Courrier's confession. Before the church wedding there had, of course, to be confession. Like most men in the village, Alphonse never went to church. Not that he was an atheist either in name, conviction or any other sense. He didn't go to church simply because it was not something men did; he belonged to that half of the parish priest's flock which grazed outside, within striking distance of the front entrance. This is not to say that there was any conflict with the shepherd — it was purely a question of how space was allocated: the etiquette of the day was very clear about it. The priest would be well received when he strayed from his appointed place to converse with the men. Once there, he would never have taken the liberty of preaching or exhorting. Anyone who wanted that sort of thing only had to cross the threshold of the church to get it in abundance.

Alphonse Courrier crossed that threshold, with all proper feelings of sincere respect, about three days before his wedding, in order, as we have said, to make his confession.

ONE

"Are you approaching the sacrament of marriage with a pure heart, my son?"

The periwinkle-blue of Alphonse Courrier's eyes rose to meet his confessor's gaze, but the elderly cleric's watery blue stood little chance against the younger man's piercing enamel. The priest was forced to lower his gaze, embarrassed at his own ritual question. What had shamed him? Absolute innocence, pointlessly provoked, or guilt so absolute that all questions were superfluous? Whichever it may have been, the fact is that – when it came to the matter of Alphonse Courrier's spiritual readiness for matrimony – the priest declined to investigate further.

"What sins do you remember and wish to confess?" he asked after a pause.

"Those are two different things," the future bridegroom replied gently.

At this age, Courrier already wore his gold-rimmed spectacles, and their gleam lit up the dark of the confessional, which was actually a corner of the vestry in the church that stood opposite the shop. The penitent was kneeling with his elbows propped comfortably on the arm-rest of the prie-dieu, one hand scratching his chin then gently kneading his shoulder beneath its light shirt. It was May, and the weather was already fairly hot.

The priest rephrased his question with a patient sigh:

"What sins are you confessing?"

He had dropped two verbs, Alphonse noted, and modified the remaining one. Things stood differently now, from a linguistic point of view. And after all, he'd come here to perform a task. To that end, he had left the shop briefly, hanging the "Back Soon" sign on the door; in those days he still had no assistants.

He took a deep breath and attempted to summon a concept of sin which might mean something both to himself and the priest. His two nights a week in the hayloft could not, to his way of thinking, be classed as a sin. It was a sin, if anything, to be relinquishing them. Now let's be clear about this, Alphonse was not using the word "sin" lightly here, as in the expression: "It'd be a sin to stop now, we were having such fun . . ." No, his opinion had much deeper roots than that – it was inseparable, for example, from the image of Adèle's face when she reached the peak of pleasure with him, on those twice-weekly occasions. But, however fundamental this subject, it would be impossible to broach it with his confessor without having to go into embarrassing explanations. Why make things difficult for the old man, when the two of them would certainly never be able to agree? Omission! That was the answer! He would omit the whole subject and, in the process, give himself something to confess. Omission was one of the sins you were supposed to declare, in fact he seemed to remember that it was fairly substantial, while being hard to describe in detail.

"My sins," he said, "have been those of omission," looking the priest in the eye. There were two possibilities: the old man would either ask what Alphonse had omitted, or move on to the next sin. At the start of any game, there will always be one player who seizes the initiative, while the other responds. It is an almost imperceptible test of the two contestants' strength, but no guarantee of victory for either. It is simply the sign of who will be dealing the cards and keeping charge of the pack;

(in his spare time, on the other evenings, Courrier used to join the cardplayers at the village inn).

"What else?" the priest asked.

So he had moved on. Well played Alphonse! Not that Courrier was trying to outwit him. I think here I ought to clarify an aspect of our man's character: he was naturally inclined to courtesy. It made him uncomfortable to embarrass others; witnessing their discomfort upset him on an aesthetic level. Which is not the same as saying that Alphonse Courrier was a good man – but I don't think there's any need to elaborate. The matter is clear enough, or, if it isn't, the course of events will make it so.

Anyway, to return to our confession. Courrier had no desire to be cruel either to the priest, who was, after all, giving up his time, or even to himself, who was stealing time from the shop. He was well aware that, for a prenuptial confession to be satisfactory, it needed something more. But what? Unlike the usual run of penitents, Courrier was not burying his face in his hands contritely, or squirming in the throws of remorse. Rather, he gazed amicably at his judge, implicitly asking for help to understand what harm he could possibly have done. Once again let me emphasise: this was not a rhetorical question. Courrier really was asking what harm he could possibly have done in his life, at least so far. For a split second he wondered whether it could be his sustained absence from the church that made him feel so innocent. He lifted his crystal-clear eyes to his confessor, who once more lowered his own and raised his hand in a blessing. That was as much as you got out of Alphonse Courrier.

TWO

His wife was Agnès Duval. She came from the neighbouring village and she was an excellent deal. It is pointless to recoil and affect shock at the word "deal". It is just the right word, and conveys the idea perfectly. Mlle Duval would have been an excellent deal for anybody, particularly anybody not in love with her since, in the labyrinthine paths of love, success can never be certain.

Alphonse Courrier faced no such danger. He did not love his future wife, so he was well placed to plan and execute a clear, logical, practical strategy. On his wedding day he was the most satisfied man on earth: a general who had led his forces to victory in a campaign of conquest. This was another element of Courrier's character: he thought of himself less as a single being than as a sum of homogeneous parts, all cooperating towards the common good and ready to sacrifice themselves for the happiness of the whole. No need to spell out, in this instance, which of his parts was sacrificing itself. As a child he too must have heard Menenius Agrippa's parable about co-operation between the limbs and the stomach; in those days primary schooling was founded on simplification and anecdote.

The families of Alphonse and Agnès approved of the match too, and cooperated willingly, and fairly, over the dowry and wedding expenses. The question on such occasions was one of quantity: who should contribute most? The girl's dowry was an inescapable obligation, decreed by the unwritten law governing marital contracts. The groom too had certain obligations, but they were vaguer and less rigid. Alphonse offered his bride an enviable position in village society, a well-established shop, a solid house (the bride would provide the linen), and furniture which may not have been exactly new, but had been very well cared for by the elder Madame Courrier, who was now beating an orderly retreat to a smaller and more private area of the same establishment.

The laws of custom dictated all this, and it would never have occurred to anybody to rebel and establish an alternative system, least of all to Agnès Duval or Alphonse Courrier – but for two entirely different reasons. In her case, because she could not have imagined her future in any other way; in his, because from here, from this safe haven, his ship of life would embark on a voyage whose basic requirement was solitude (defined here as an absence of obstacles). It is no simple task to prepare for such a journey, to build a harbour from which to set sail. He had to give the impression of stability to those who were to stay behind, unaware of the fact that he had weighed anchor.

On the day of the wedding, as he stepped into the church to wait for his bride, Alphonse felt the cheerfulness of the traveller who is eager to be under sail. He had slept soundly the night before and had, with difficulty, foregone breakfast, to comply with the fast that Communion required. He had had to be reminded of this by his mother, who, unlike Alphonse, was well practised in such matters.

He was very well dressed. He had not the slightest interest in what his bride would be wearing. Popular superstition demanded silence on the subject; a series of rituals required the groom to be totally ignorant of the bride's dress. This must have been a vestige of a more complete ignorance, from the days when a groom was not permitted to see his bride's face or, most importantly, her body. None of this mattered very

17

much to Alphonse Courrier. He knew her face well enough and he would discover her body, without any great surprises, in due course. As he waited for Agnès, he was more interested in the village as a whole.

Since he wasn't nervous, and since everybody assumed he must be, he was in the perfect position to observe. He was standing next to the altar, up to which he would eventually lead his fiancée, and looking towards the main doorway: a rectangle of light which framed the guests as they entered the church, a few at a time. They, naturally, believed they were there to look at him – him and her, to be precise – but, since he was the one who had orchestrated the event, Alphonse felt as if he had summoned them there for his own enjoyment. He was examining them, these guests of his, away from the shop where he was used to seeing them, in the unaccustomed gloom of a dark nave, the temporary master of a space which was not his own.

For the most part they struck him as ugly; comical and ugly. A village in its Sunday best is an unprepossessing sight. Looking provisional in their borrowed masks, the guests lent the day a feeling of the most complete artificiality. A girl came in, alone, and dressed up in keeping with the occasion. She came forward through the half-light, searching for a seat at the end of a row, where she could get a good view of the bride's entrance. Courrier, standing at the altar, studied her intently. His glasses, fortunately, somewhat concealed the direction of his gaze. She sat down rather rigidly, without leaning back in her seat, put her feet up on the kneeler, and clasped her bag on her lap with both hands. She was staring straight ahead but, you can be sure, saw nothing: there is nothing to see until the entrance of the bride.

And enter she did: a very fine presence, in just the right dress. She was followed by the benevolent gaze of the whole congregation, including the solitary girl half-way down the nave. When we draw a line between three points, we end up with a triangle. The three points of our particular triangle were as follows: the periwinkle-blue of Courrier's eyes; a pair of nondescript brown pupils half-way down the nave; and the quiet blue of the bride's own gaze. The periwinkle touched the brown, which reached out to the blue, which in turn went back to meet the periwinkle. That is how a triangle is drawn. In case anybody should think of this as a prelude to adultery, let me correct them immediately: the motive behind that first gaze was entirely different. Also quite different were Alphonse Courrier's thoughts as he drew that first side of the triangle: I think that, more than anything else in the world, he was fascinated by ugliness.

The start of the ceremony found him distracted, but he quickly adjusted himself or, rather, adjusted the mask of his face (an excellent shield, this, which his glasses subtly reinforced until it was well-nigh impregnable). Before being dragged in to those ritual formulas which required a coherent answer from him, he had the whole of the first part of the service in which to elaborate certain private theories. These, broadly speaking, related to the link between man and the apes.

THREE

They were a symptom of the Darwinian climate of the day –
I am referring to Courrier's thoughts about apes – but that
wasn't the whole story. It is true that, in his own small way,
Alphonse Courrier was a reader, but he was not easily influ-
enced by fashion; even less by other people's opinions. His
simian conclusions had been reached entirely on his own,
guided, if at all, by the girl sitting half-way down the nave; but
even she acted as no more than a tangible starting-point.

All of us descend from the apes; Courrier felt certain of that.
The only exception he might make was himself: a man whose
looks did not instantly call to mind the lower primates. But
these others, these villagers dressed up in honour of his
wedding, looked like some living catalogue that the English
scientist might have used for his theses. The more tidily and
sedately they sat, purged of work-day slovenliness in their
starched clothes, the stronger this resemblance became.

As the priest went on with the service, the groom – eyes half-
closed to see better into his memory – focused one at a time
on a series of faces, including that of the girl half-way down
the nave. The black silk of her dress covered a stocky body
and afforded a glimpse of her thick ankles. At the opposite
end, an equally powerful neck supported her heavy head, which
was emphasised by thick, dark hair. She had adorned herself
as best she could: a silver necklace besieged her neck, upon
which also rested a shiny double chin. Her mouth hung half-
open with a mixture of wonder and emotion. But then the

well-dressed, attractive woman standing next to him was just as much a descendant of the apes as that girl; Courrier was sure of this. It was only a matter of a few years – even now, all it needed was a little imagination – before she would wither into the old age already apparent in his mother, sitting just behind them in the front row. Some very youthful faces carry latent signs of their future selves, for which their present beauty acts only as a flimsy mask. Agnès Duval was one of those. The girl half-way down the nave, by contrast, was defenceless, and could be read like a book. That was why Courrier could not get her out of his mind. It was like staring at some deformity of the skin and feeling simultaneously fascinated and repelled.

Monkeys, however, are less ridiculous. They are not, for instance, in the habit of hiding their bodies with clothes. Neither do they ostentatiously celebrate natural occurrences, such as copulation. Nobody called it that, of course, but what else was it? All things have a name, all animals a body, all functions a cause and an effect. Man's passage across the face of this earth – across it and beyond – is the most basic process there is; by leaving a physical trace of himself, he feels this passage has not been in vain. That was the reason for all this ritual, this enthronement.

And indeed he was now sitting on a kind of diminutive red velvet throne, his future wife at his side. Future? For a moment he felt disorientated. Did "future" mean in five minutes' time? He stole a glance at the watch he kept in the pocket of the waistcoat he was wearing for the occasion – heavy material at the front and pearl-grey satin at the back. It suited him; the neatness of the trimmings allowed it to be worn without a jacket when necessary. There were less than five minutes to go. They seemed to have drawn very close to the event while his thoughts were wandering around the nave. The girl at his side probably had more of a grip on the situation: she, most likely, had been paying attention. Courrier pulled himself together; he had been in danger of weighing anchor too early.

And, sure enough, at that moment the rings appeared. It still wasn't quite time, however. From an unseen corner of the church, some functionary had dispatched two children, bearing the gold circles on a small cushion, and now they stood behind the protagonists, ready to pounce. They were in fancy dress too, poor little creatures. Even the children. The offspring of man, they suffered the consequences of sartorial vanity as soon as they had use of their legs. In rich families it started even earlier; they dolled them up when they still had no control over their limbs, still less their bodily functions – the result, more often than not, disaster.

Courrier remembered the time when the village noblewoman (so to speak), gave birth to her first male child. She used to take the baby out in a perambulator with four enormous wheels and a wicker basket decorated like a Christmas hamper. Through the ribbons and the Valencienne lace there peeped – or at times you had to burrow through yards of material to find – a little wrinkled face, all red with the effort of birth and of endeavouring not to drown in frills. Not an inch of his skin was spared suffocation, entombed as he was in the attentions of the adult world, a world which seemed to hide him away for the pleasure of unveiling him again. Or perhaps his mother and grandmother may have been right in their determination to keep him out of sight: to the impartial eye the little chap was, frankly, ugly. As he grew up they continued to conceal him under mountains of material and, sure enough, his ugliness persisted.

The boy was standing behind Courrier at that very moment. As a special favour, his family had allowed him to serve as a ring-bearer for the ceremony. The girl beside him was no more of a beauty than he was; pallid of eye and face, engrossed in her role, she glanced at her companion in secret anticipation.

The small couple saw itself reflected in the adult one. Courrier found it easy to reward them both with a sincere smile when they held out the red cushion and its golden rings.

Rings which, shortly afterwards, were sparkling on the fingers of man and wife. The childish couple had separated, returning to the anonymity of the pews, and an indelible adult couple had been formed. It had taken no more than a moment. A brief formula, barely audible from the front rows (the girl half-way down the nave certainly wouldn't have heard a thing) and Alphonse Courrier ceased to be alone in the world. All calculated to perfection – yet, for a fraction of a second, he felt giddy. The possibility of that something – that crazed variable – skewing the rules of the game and wrong-footing its players flashed through his mind. He turned in fear to the stranger at his side and saw her smile calmly, her expression barely veiled by a hint of emotion. He was gripped by the suspicion that this woman, Agnès Duval, might be even more calculating than he was. A woman's coldness can far exceed a man's rationality, since it is born of a deeper knowledge of life. Totally lacking in theory, it heeds only concrete results.

She was still smiling. Courrier noticed that his bride's gums grew low over her teeth, so that her smile uncovered an area of pink which he had never noticed before. He responded with a tight-lipped smile. Peasant culture, sober and reserved, did not allow for the newlyweds to kiss on the mouth, which was just as well. The guests saw to it that the bride's cheeks were covered in kisses as soon as she left the church. For his part, Courrier received embraces, handshakes, and the odd salacious remark, which he accepted with the cheerful composure of a man who had already crossed certain thresholds.

Courrier did not find the reception too wearying, even though it went on till late. As for afterwards, he slept as easily as he had on the previous night. Perhaps even better: in the first place because he really was tired, and secondly because the step he had taken filled him with the quiet satisfaction which comes with completing one leg of a journey. The following day was a Sunday; the shop would remain shut; his new life was beginning in the most auspicious of ways. Another reason for sleeping soundly could have been the carrying out of his conjugal duties, but why fulfil them according to the standards and expectations of others? The village had sought to solemnise this copulation, and the village had been satisfied. As for Courrier, he had his whole life ahead of him, and slept all the more soundly for it. The next morning Agnès Duval was still Agnès Duval – Madame Courrier only in the eyes of Mother Church and the Town Hall.

FOUR

Humanity does not comprehend benevolence. Perhaps we did at the beginning of time, when individuals saw themselves reflected in their fellow men, and probably felt a great need for them. So much so that they began to talk about "treating someone with humanity". Today it would be better if nobody were prone to this emotion, precisely because it is so far removed from benevolence. This observation, made in a remote corner of the Auvergne, is not in the least odd. One starting point is as good as any other, and Courrier's opinions were not to be despised – particularly this one, which was about benevolence, not goodness.

Once Courrier had sampled married life in depth – which took him no more than two or three weeks, because he was a shrewd man, and farsighted, especially when it came to detail, he was a past master when it came to detail, and second to nobody, always, even as a child, he had considered details essential to an understanding of the whole – but, as I was saying, two, or at most three, weeks of married life confirmed his suspicion that he was going to have to keep to himself his thoughts on humanity and benevolence and, similarly, to withhold benevolence itself.

Morning. The breakfast table was neatly laid, by an expert hand; warm milk in his cup; the bread, if not exactly fresh (surely nobody, no matter how rich, could expect fresh bread every day!) was full of flavour, and the home-made jam was better even than his mother's. While he was spreading the apple jam on his bread and it was still dark outside – in that transition between night and day, cradled in the bosom of his family, it occurred to Courrier that he had married a harpy.

A harpy is a mythical beast which prophesied that Aeneas and his men would one day be so famished, they would be forced to eat their plates. It was this prophecy which led to the invention of the *focaccia* or – less accurately – the sandwich. There she sat, his harpy, passing him slices of bread to spread with apple jam. The best woman in the world, who looked after her husband (by this time, after two or three weeks, he really was her husband and she really was Madame Alphonse Courrier) and ran her household with decorum, so that, in the eyes of the village, the rite performed in church was confirmed as an excellent transaction – one that could be reassessed day by day, like an income from land or property. A real harpy! But if any of you is thinking that this conclusion, reached one morning over bread and jam, was a bitter one, you are mistaken. We are not dealing with a starry-eyed idealist, but a man who – sitting at the table with his legs crossed and smoking a good cigar, the taste of apple jam still on his lips – had a realistic attitude and definite ideas. A rare breed, and an example to anyone involved in politics – politics in its broadest sense, of course, meaning social relations and worldly wisdom. It all depended on how one understood the word "harpy"; because Courrier, when it came to his view on the excellence of his marital investment, had not retreated an inch. He had made his decision, and he was sure it was for the best.

They say nobody is perfect, but everybody is endlessly searching for perfection. It must be born, this search, of our innate conviction that within ourselves – hidden to others, but for the most part visible to us – we harbour just such perfection. The rest of the world cannot see it, any more than it can see a vein of gold buried in a mountainside. The base rock surrounding the precious metal acts as its defence against brutal plunder. This is the way with gold; but in much the same way, some people assume they have to defend their perfection tooth and nail, and do all they can to conceal it, to the point of stifling it altogether. "Better dead and unmolested than alive and ravished" seems to be, roughly speaking, their attitude. An attitude which was not suited to Alphonse Courrier, but was to Agnès Duval. Very much so. The reasons it did not suit Courrier were, firstly, that he suffered from claustrophobia, so the very idea of stifling anything made him feel ill; and, secondly, that he had no perfection to hide: his was plainly visible for all to see. That, believe it or not, was the source of his benevolence. And that – it hardly needs stating – was the source of his wife's malevolence. Which is not to say she was bad. The last person to make such a mistaken assumption would have been Alphonse, who did not love her, and therefore could never misread the situation so grossly.

As he inhaled his last mouthful of smoke, on that same apple-jam morning, Courrier thanked heaven (heaven in general, without singling out any one of its potential inhabitants), that he did not love Agnès Duval. Then he kissed the smooth forehead that came up to the level of his chin (he might almost have taken her measurements before marrying her!), watched the pink of her ample gums being uncovered by her smile, and left the house in his shirt sleeves, just as dawn was breaking on a summer's day. He was in his shirt sleeves because every evening he left behind, in the shop, the black overalls which enrobed him as he worked. At a guess it was sometime in June.

At this point we ought to have a nice description of June in the Auvergne, because it would be worth it, in case any of you never got the chance to see it. The village was so encircled by fields, so cosily nestled into the hills. But Alphonse Courrier's thoughts were not proceeding in that direction, so to venture there ourselves, in a digression, would perhaps be rather indelicate. The fact remains that it was undeniably a beautiful June, but we will leave it at that.

Courrier, in the meantime, had raised the metal blind on his shop door, entered his kingdom, and calmly begun to reconsider certain details.

FIVE

Detail one: in the evenings, before going to bed, Agnès prayed. This was not a habit shared by her husband, either in the sense of sharing that particular moment with her and joining in, or in the sense of sharing the beliefs behind the practice – about which, however, he expressed no particular opinion, either for or against. He did not pray; she did. That might have been the end of the matter, except of course that he had to witness her evening ceremony. They slept in the same room, in the same bed, so the night-time rituals of the one were performed under the nose of the other.

First, she would comb her hair thoroughly – no, her very first step was to undress with intricate manoeuvres designed to hide any glimpse of bare flesh from her husband. After that she combed her hair, as I was saying, and it was a long, solitary, deliberately excluding, operation. Finally she prayed, or "gathered her thoughts", as people say. That is, she shrank back in on herself and shrivelled up into a state of sly contrition. (No, there is no mistake there, that does say "sly".) She pressed her nose between her hands, closed her eyes, and even appeared to stop breathing. She didn't leave the smallest chink for the world to squeeze through. Her ears, undefended, presumably equipped themselves with some kind of mental insulation. The first time he witnessed this, Courrier couldn't resist an impulse to murmur something and watch her head turn fractionally towards him, only to correct itself immediately and stiffen even further.

Courrier was not upset or rendered jealous by this exclusion: he was sure that his wife's head remained perfectly empty as her memory accurately recited a sequence of words. If she'd been suffering from toothache, there would have been some justification for all of this grieving. But, judging from the way she had been brushing her hair only minutes before, no pain, or memory of pain, was troubling her. All the more proof of her excellent acting abilities, Diderot would have said. Now, I don't know if Courrier had read "Paradox on Acting", but he and Denis Diderot would have found themselves in agreement on her performance: Diderot full of admiration, Courrier with a few reservations – not so much concerning the standard of the performance, as the necessity for it.

Out of a desire to oppose her – since opposition is at the heart of all things – Courrier felt moved to lie down and sprawl on the bed. He did at least have enough tact to repress the sigh of satisfaction which was about to escape him.

Detail two: Madame Courrier ate. An operation which, in their house, took place on average three times a day, in a crescendo of complexity which reached its peak in the evening. At that hour three of them sat down to a well-stocked table, to which the younger Madame Courrier had contributed as cook and the older Madame Courrier as commentator. Alphonse, the third diner, arrived when the die, so to speak, had been cast. Whatever may have been said in the kitchen, for good or ill, he did not discern even as a distant echo. As for what had been done, his verdict was always favourable, and with good reason: the younger Madame Courrier was an excellent cook.

I was saying that Agnès Courrier ate. Apart from the merest hint of impropriety while drinking (that slight sucking noise – a charge on which he himself was not innocent), her manners were impeccable. She must have been taught certain rules which, once mastered, she applied with judicious ease. It was just that she was meticulous in the extreme about finishing off her food: not a grain of rice ever remained on the edge of her plate; not a drop of broth in the bottom of her bowl; nor was there even the merest hint of sauce which her bread did not wipe up systematically, again and again. And then there was the matter of the breadcrumbs.

When nothing else was left, in defiance of etiquette – or perhaps nobody had ever warned her about this – Agnès would use the tip of her finger as a sort of suction device to collect the last of the crumbs. Sometimes, when she was confronted with a larger mass, she proceeded in the same way, but holding all the fingers of one hand together and capturing little mounds of bread which she would then pop into her mouth with the enjoyment of a woman who has done her duty. Like a Stoic (if unaware of her adherence to a philosophical school), Madame Courrier combined pleasure and practicality to the full satisfaction of her conscience.

As Courrier sat in his quiet shop, early in the morning, sorting nails and screws into boxes and drawers under the counter, he could have listed at least five or six more details in which he had become expert since beginning married life. The way she relayed the village gossip; the way she insinuated things with questions rather than making statements; the keen way she watched people in the street through the window; the way she worked at broadening her knowledge of the houses opposite, translating it into an insistent monologue: "Germaine will be out in a minute . . . She's going to have to take that washing in soon . . Surely she's not going to wait till it's bone dry . . ." etc.

His half-extinguished cigar dangling from his lips, Courrier narrowed his eyes into blue slits and looked out through the door at that section of the village square which lay under his nose from dawn till dusk.

"Alphonse, this blade won't do. I did the field below the church only a couple of times and it's already blunt."

Monsieur Courrier turned towards his first customer of the day: the peasant who tended the priest's orchard. He took the sickle from him, ran an expert finger across the blade, and set to work. In the meantime his customer dawdled around the shop for a while, then picked up a pair of shiny new scissors from the end of the counter and tested them for sharpness.

"God damn it, Alphonse! You've not skimped on these!" he commented, and sucked his bleeding thumb.

"Want them?" Monsieur Courrier asked coolly as he handed back the perfectly sharpened sickle.

"How much do I owe you?" asked the customer, without removing his bleeding finger from his lips.

"With the scissors, a franc. Without them, nothing." And, as the other man reached into his pocket, he added, "Pay me next time. There's no hurry." But the coin was already on the counter, and the scissors passed over to the buyer.

"You'll clean the blood off them yourself, won't you?" Courrier said with a wink.

"Goodbye," the man replied. "If you're coming out this evening, I'll buy you a drink."

Alphonse Courrier was thoroughly well-liked. When it came to village gossip, he knew a lot more than his wife, but he didn't pass it on to her.

The world (meaning both the terraqueous globe and a small village in the Auvergne) is really not that vast. You can get around it tolerably quickly, more often than not meeting old friends along the way, or friends of friends with whom Chance delights in weaving connections. This phenomenon shortens distances even more, but in such a way that those who experience these tricks and repetitions of time feel as if they are living through a strange adventure; something exceptional.

Thus, in this world of ours, does the norm disguise itself.

From his shop, as I was saying, Courrier could see all the village go by. Go by, and come in. After the peasant had left with his scissors and sharpened sickle, the next person to appear in the doorway was the priest's housekeeper – a woman whose age was sufficiently advanced to satisfy church regulations, but who had lost none of the somewhat brazen charms of her youth. Odd for such a woman to be the curé's housekeeper? Not as odd as the truth, which was that she loved him like a father and went further afield to indulge her carnal desires, to the extent of venturing beyond the village – whose population disbelieved her virtue to a man. Not even Agnès believed it. Alphonse Courrier did, but he let his wife's tittle-tattle weave a fine web of poison around the beautiful forty-year-old. Virtue shines especially brightly when vilified.

"I wouldn't like to be in Germaine's shoes when she tries to iron that dry laundry. Surely everyone knows the sun is hottest at noon. I know it. My mother taught me not to waste time and effort around the house."

It was midday, and Alphonse was home from the shop. Agnès was still exercising herself about the laundry technique of the neighbour across the street, and about the neighbour across the street in general.

As he sat waiting for his lunch at the kitchen table, the man of the house reflected that he had married a very capable woman – able and poisonous – as he'd been bound to do. Here too, although the light from the window was not particularly bright, Courrier narrowed his eyes to blue slits and watched, beyond his wife's full curves, the outline of Germaine on her way back to the house with a basket of laundry which – as anyone could have predicted – was bone dry.

SIX

Night, for Courrier, was a blackboard on which he sketched the observations he had made during the day. He suffered from insomnia or, to be more precise, he occasionally found it hard to get to sleep, but it caused him no suffering. On the contrary, his night-time vigil revealed horizons which the day did not, and, in the darkness that loomed before his open eyes, he chalked up a host of ideas. He was not a gossip, but he knew a lot about the people around him. The night was perfect for pondering the events of the day: the silence of the house, his wife's breathing beside him, (a breathing which time would render increasingly powerful until it came to merit a different name), and the protection of a sheet pulled up to his chin, cutting him off from the rest of the room. Never, even in the hottest of summers, would he have slept without a sheet.

The peculiarity of this nocturnal blackboard was that it could not be wiped clean. Once something had been written, it remained for ever. If it were possible for us to decipher, it would reveal an interesting world which, over many nights, had amassed a wealth of detail. Germaine's basket, for instance, and the reason for her negligence over fetching the washing; or her slightly melancholy, cross-eyed gaze, which brought her no admirers. Sooner or later, she too would get married. No man in the village could permit himself the luxury of being without a woman to keep house, and a melancholy, cross-eyed man in the mould of Germaine could always be found – or, if not, there would always be one in some nearby village, where word of the girl's scant charms would certainly have arrived. A less damning reputation by far than any she might acquire in relation to her bad housekeeping.

The jewel of perfection who lay asleep at Courrier's side was the yardstick against which the poor young woman opposite could be measured. How she struggled, and to what little effect! From some mysterious motive, somewhat akin to kindness of heart, Courrier decided to go to her assistance. The church bell in the village square tolled three in the morning as Alphonse was drawing up his plan of action. Great generals are often insomniacs.

SEVEN

In literature, everything has already been written. There is no
situation which has not been dealt with, read and filed away.
Quotations abound; stories recur. The same goes for History
itself. The lives of, if not the first man, certainly the first hundred,
would be enough to contain nearly every existence which, over
the centuries, individuals have believed they were living out for
the very first time. Luckily historical memory is barely sufficient
to cover the great events, and ignores the small ones altogether,
leaving the illusion, each time something happens, that nobody
has ever experienced such a thing – good or bad – before. Not
like this, anyway. And in those two words: like this, the whole of
human life is written.

Courrier was not a historian, or even an average reader of
history. At most he might glance over the current affairs pages
in the newspapers. He was not really at home with books in
general, and he knew nothing of ancient poetry, except the *Iliad*.
He had never even heard the names of Dido and Aeneas, or the
story of the hunt and the thunderstorm, and the cave where
each – ignorant of the other's presence – took shelter, allowing
Fate to play itself out on them. Ignorant – up to a point.

Courrier refused to go hunting on principle, so this may not
be a very apt comparison, but there was a thunderstorm, and
the gloom of his shop – particularly in the back, which the light
from the windows hardly reached, even on sunny days – might
be compared to that of a cave in the Libyan forest, beneath the
fury of the elements. Germaine, naturally, was not frightened

by the storm, but braving such torrential rain was too much even for a robust country girl like her, and it so happened that the cave-cum-shop offered timely shelter. It was all pure chance: the golden blond of Courrier's face in the shadows; the flash of his eyes behind the gold-rimmed lenses; the deserted square behind her (everyone else had prudently retreated indoors when the rain started) and the silence, the utter silence of a village where normal life was suspended as everyone waited for the end of the storm. Courrier was not the sort of man to feel Aeneas' doubts, yet, on this occasion, he did not take things as far as those two lovers did in ancient times. That was not his aim. At some point, he was sure, ugly Germaine would have a husband, and it would not be wise to pre-empt that experience. What she would never have, on the other hand, was the sensation of making a man fall in love with her; a man who would look at her with intensity, with tenderness, with a passion which had to be suppressed because the law forbade an emotion which his heart would gladly have given and received. This was the feeling he wanted to offer, as a gift, to ugly Germaine.

Her hair was soaked through and plastered against her neck, and there was a lost expression in her eyes. In one dripping hand she clutched the large key to her front door. She bounded through the shop doorway, then recoiled with shyness when her eyes met the owner's gaze. For a moment she felt tempted to retreat into the rain. Courrier was masterly. He lowered his eyes and pretended to search for something in the till, allowing the girl to reassure herself that she had not disturbed him. Then he slid the till drawer shut noisily and fixed his gaze on her as she stood with her back to the cave, watching the rain with the look of someone who meant to leave as soon as it showed signs of easing. Courrier stared at her as if his eyes could project heat on to the back of her neck. He must have managed to project something because, at long last, she tore herself away from the rain, moved a little further under cover, and gave Courrier a timid smile of gratitude. He returned it, then came out from behind the counter and produced a short wooden step-ladder, the one he used to reach the lower shelves. He opened it out and offered it to the girl as a stool.

"It won't stop for a while yet. Come and sit down, Germaine."

His visitor was no longer a child, but it seemed natural to use her first name because of the way she always looked guilty, as if she would find a little familiarity reassuring.

"Please don't let me disturb you, Monsieur Courrier. Please go on with your accounts."

Monsieur Courrier drew close to her, to check whether the rain was performing as required. In one hand he was holding the open step-ladder, which he set down in a dark corner of the shop.

"I'll do my books, but you sit down. You'll be out of the rain here," he said, indicating what amounted to a sort of crevasse, where nobody would notice her, even if they peered in through the door. The square was still deserted; the storm was spreading out, darkening the narrow sections of hill which could be seen between the houses.

"Are you on your way home from the fields?"

"Yes."

"You waited too long, did you?"

She replied with a frightened smile.

"Good. If you weren't in a hurry before, then you needn't be now. This won't stop for at least an hour. Will they be expecting you at home?"

"No, they know I can look after myself."

"Why are you calling me 'Monsieur Courrier'? Don't you like 'Alphonse'? I know it's not a very nice name . . ." Suddenly he looked distant, lost in who knows what thoughts. He lit his cigar; its tip burnt red, like a heart against his lips. Germaine was not given to poetic imagery, but something similar must have occurred to her, and she looked at him in a new light.

"Germaine isn't very pretty either," she ventured, her eyes lowered to hide her wayward pupils. She was comforted by the thought that the half-light would disguise her abnormality. If only she could have had his steady, laughing, periwinkle eyes. How they laughed! At that moment, Courrier seemed – how can I put it? – extraordinarily close. Now he was the one who was standing at the door, watching the rain. He had his back to her, and he seemed to have forgotten all about her.

"It's lucky you ended up here, Germaine," he said suddenly.

"It certainly is, Monsieur – Alphonse," she replied. "I couldn't have made it home."

He turned round and stared at her with a strange look, which Germaine found hard to interpret. Had she misunderstood? Lucky for whom? Then he smiled at her – his barely parted lips holding his cigar safely in place – and came closer. He stroked her hair.

"So very wet, my girl . . . " he stopped, his hand hovering in mid air.

Germaine had had no notion of what it meant to feel an intense gaze or, rather, had not until that moment. The emotion which stirred within her then, no refined lover, no connoisseur of pleasure would ever arouse in her again. (I should mention, in passing, that Germaine did not go on to marry a connoisseur of pleasure, but a robust peasant who thought first and foremost of himself.) In any case, that moment – that hand poised inches from her body – marked her soul. To tell the truth it marked Alphonse Courrier too: he couldn't remember a time when his acting had risen so magnificently to the occasion, and beyond.

When the girl stepped out of the shop into the light drizzle which was the final legacy of the storm's violence, the shop-keeper watched her go with tenderness in his eyes. There was no pretence this time, no deceit. He saw her pick her way gingerly through the puddles without a backward glance, giving nothing away: to all appearances, the same person as before.

Courrier re-lit his cigar and narrowed his eyes, enjoying the half-light of the early dusk brought on by the thunderstorm. What was the name of that first girl in the hayloft? Adèle? She too walked calmly beneath the eyes of the world. The shop-keeper puffed out his cheeks and, ever so softly, blew a low whistle of satisfaction.

EIGHT

Those first hundred men – the ones who experienced everything that others were to relive over the centuries – those men
also probably possessed all, or almost all, the faces to be seen
in future generations. Without wishing to detract from the
inventiveness of Our Father (to whom Courrier, from outside
the church, bowed with his usual politeness, and the respect
for other's views to which he was naturally inclined), without
wishing to detract from Him, as I was saying, there had been
nothing new under the sun since time immemorial. Perhaps it
wasn't even His intention that there should have been.

Let us by all means admit that Alphonse Courrier's shop was
a rather restricted observatory (the image of the observatory is
one which is favoured by many people who think, mistakenly,
that it sounds both scientific and alchemical. Most of those
who use it have never set foot in an observatory – they never
even look out of their own windows, except to admire their
reflection). The people who passed by his door were usually
from the village; the few outsiders were not from very far away
and had nothing much to distinguish them. So it was not
surprising that everyone should look similar. But once, a few
years before – before his marriage, I mean – Courrier had spent
two days in Paris. One might argue that two days is a very short
time, but for this young provincial from the Auvergne it was
long enough to form some sort of impression. What difference
was there between the people who drank in the inn opposite
his shop and those in a bistrot on the banks of the Seine? Some

of the Parisians looked sicklier, others more condescending (although there were people in the village who weren't short of arrogance either), but in every other respect they were exactly the same. It was during this visit that he invented and perfected a private game, which came to fascinate him: scrutinising people's faces and bearing for more and more examples of types he had encountered elsewhere.

Two days in Paris is a very short time. He spent them – once he had concluded the business which had brought him there and which need not concern us – observing the people of the city. His future wife would have done the same, wallowing in what, to her, would have seemed a limitless ocean of dresses. On closer inspection, however, there was no great variety in that area either.

"Whichever way you look at it, naked we're born and naked we die!" proclaimed Alphonse. No, he did not address these words to his wife. She would have raised her eyebrows in indignation and shrunk away from the nudity her husband purported to see all around, even in her. Good Lord! At times she had the feeling she'd married a – if she had known the word, she could have said a provocateur. But she did not know it.

It was to his fellow card-players that Courrier had allowed himself to voice this thought. They met at the inn every Saturday evening – a mixed group, both in terms of age and social standing. Occasionally they were even joined by the mayor or the veterinary surgeon, who came over from a nearby village where no decent Scopa-playing groups had formed. Scopa is a game that can be found all over Europe, whatever name it goes by in the various countries; a game of wits, not chance.

In cards, as in other things, Courrier had a certain style. He would pretend to ignore the rest of the table, remaining pensive and aloof. He took his time to play his card, seeming to choose it at random out of the fan which slid expertly between his fingers, then he would wait for his companions' reaction. They always played in silence – a web of glances communicating the mood of the players – except for the explosion of fury from the loser of each round, or the bewilderment of a player who thought he'd made it, only to be thrown by an opponent's self-control.

"Naked we're born and naked we die. We can wear as many clothes as we want in between, but it makes no difference."

Courrier tossed the thought down on to the table, together with a queen of spades that swept the board. Cardplayers do not usually pay much attention to this sort of reflection: they know that games are always peppered with amateur philosophy and witty asides, in an environment where all tends to be forgiven. But this particular remark, accompanied as it was by the queen of spades, made the vet think. A passionate, meticulous player, he paused for a moment, pack in hand, while dealing for the next round; the last had been won by Courrier. Then he started dealing again and, without taking his eyes off the cards, muttered between his teeth:

"In a bad mood are we, Alphonse?"

"Never better, Doctor, never better. The more I think about these things, the happier I am. Happy with my lot. This lot or another, it's all the same to me. This face or another, I couldn't care less. There must be at least three hundred other Courriers knocking around in the world, all exactly the same – I suppose their spectacle frames may vary."

"I wouldn't throw an ace of hearts away just yet, if I were you," the grocer commented, seeing his neighbour's opening card. "But it's down now – we all know the rules." So did the vet, who had bungled his opening thanks to Courrier's wit.

"Ever since you married, my dear Courrier," he said, "you

seem to come out with this sort of thing all the time. Women help you think, I've always said that. Wives do, anyway. The other kind have a different effect."

Courrier won the game, unfairly, by breaking his opponents' concentration. Then, contemplating the dregs of a bottle of wine, whose contents they had divided between the four of them – not enough to get drunk on – he concluded his conversation with the vet, who had all night to walk back over the hill which separated his village from that of his three companions.

By now it was late July, which meant that, although the inn eventually closed for the night, the square had plenty of space to accommodate the two players and their conversation. Courrier had brought the shop keys with him, just in case, and so it was that, in the middle of the night, the people who slept over the square heard the squeal of the grille being pulled up and then, equally loud in the total silence, the sound of chairs being set out on the doorstep. On a night like that it would have been criminal to talk inside.

NINE

Towards morning, with the first saffron light of dawn, the vet left the square. He had waited politely for Courrier to lock up the shop and go home (for appearances only, given the hour); then he had set off up the hill at a brisk pace, in case a farm needed his services.

"Anyway Alphonse, it isn't true that we're born naked and die naked. We all go to the grave in our Sunday best. My father had one jacket he never wore: it was kept specially for that. I can still remember how smart he looked, lying there with his cuffs pulled down neatly and his buttons all done up – which was something he never did: he always left his jackets unbuttoned. He looked very handsome, lying there. Oh, and don't forget: just in case you're not covered enough, they put you in a coffin too! We're a very prudish race, my dear fellow, very prudish."

The vet was mulling over their night-time conversation as he walked up the white road and looked down over Courrier's village, huddled at the bottom of the valley. Everything is relative in this world of ours, he had concluded. Everything depends on your terms of comparison. Marie is more beautiful than Annette, but if you're comparing her to Agnès Duval, then Marie is less. The vet remembered that Agnès Duval was now Madame Courrier: a beautiful term of comparison, and one who was hardly ever mentioned by her husband. Silence can sometimes indicate jealousy but, on reflection, he didn't believe that this was the case with his friend. A man who has been married for three months or so – it could be a little less or a little more – and spends a whole night philosophising with the vet from the neighbouring village is not jealous – not even of his wife's thoughts, or of her solitude. Because when you're alone, your thoughts can run away with you . . .

"I've never seen anyone dressed for the next world," Alphonse had said. "Odd, isn't it? At my age I still haven't had a real death in the family. It's an experience I lack. Maybe that's why I said . . . On the other hand, you know as well as I do that the smartest jacket in the world won't stop you being naked. And prudish races are really longing to come out into the open; they're prudish because they're insecure; they're afraid they won't be able to distinguish between what is and what is not done. The truth is we're just a bundle of forgotten habits, doctor."

At the bottom of the valley, all you could still make out was the dark tip of the church tower, which at the next corner would be out of sight, to be replaced by his own village belltower. The sun was rising ahead of him, shedding its light on human insecurity. He smiled to himself as he thought of how a slight adjustment in syntax could raise the tone of a conversation. It all depends on the terms of comparison. "Human insecurity" sounds more elevated than "an insecure race". He was far from stupid, that ironmonger, casting out such innocent-looking bait, and using it to lure his companion to unexpected shores.

To tell the truth, another unexpected shore was Agnès Duval – the envied wife of that strange, enviable husband. She came from a place immediately to the north of the vet's own village, which she had passed through on the way to her wedding. The vet was elderly and, for various reasons, a bachelor, and at the time he had reflected that he wouldn't have minded if her horses had reared up and bolted with the wedding procession. But the horses had behaved impeccably and Alphonse Courrier had gained his consort, on time, in

46

front of the altar. For some reason he now gave the impression that he would be just as happy without her. Or might the vet be mistaken? Here too, he noticed the gravity of the word "consort", as compared to "wife". Courrier, the vet reflected, had no use for a consort. Life is so fascinating that a wise man would never choose to sharecrop it.

By spending so much time with peasants, he realized, he was starting to speak their language. Sharecropping was hardly a concept appropriate to this sphere of thought. He was starting down the slope into his village, and it was already too light for there to be any hope of finding it deserted.

As for Courrier, he too saw the "rosy-fingered dawn", as it was called in the old Greek poems they made him read at school. He noticed it as he passed under Germaine's window, and he cast a brief, tender glance towards the bolted shutters and the girl's closed eyes. Perhaps sleep remoulded her cross-eyed mask of a face into something more attractive . . . Lack of sleep, on the other hand, lent the beautiful Agnès a hint of grimness. Courrier too, like the vet on his way home, concluded that everything is relative, and depends on the terms of comparison.

TEN

The year was 1903. Alphonse Courrier was a man of thirty-six, with a well-established hardware business, an extremely stable home, and a son who – no, hang on, he had no son as yet. At his side, Agnès Duval took excellent care of the household, which had recently lost a member: old Madame Courrier. It happened at the beginning of 1903. When the old lady had sensed it was time to hand over the reins to an able, trusted daughter-in-law, she had gently passed away. That was how the priest had put it, during the funeral oration he gave in the same church where Alphonse's wedding had been celebrated. But the tongue of a priest on such occasions is as mendacious (or, to be precise, as unintentionally misleading) as any tongue one could possibly imagine.

Anyway, in that year of 1903, at the beginning of January, old Madame Courrier felt it necessary to begin her decline. I am calling her "old" purely in relation to her position within the family, because in fact she was a woman of not yet fifty-seven who had lived well, until that moment at least. Lived well, in the sense that she had borne only one son, had worked exclusively in the house – never in the fields – and, most importantly, had always ruled like a queen. This was the crux of the matter. The mechanisms of government – whether of a house or of a country – quickly become addictive, and can be hard to relinquish. No old age can be expected to withstand such circumstances. It is a case of exile or death (though the one often leads to the other). Madame Courrier – old Madame

Courrier – after wavering for a while between the two, must have made, deep within herself, the only possible choice: the only choice compatible with her nature. Of course, I may be misreading the situation; perhaps things did not happen quite that way.

All in all, Madame Georges Courrier appeared to be a meek woman. The meek are the most terrifying race ever to have walked this earth, and one untroubled by fear of extinction. The word "race" may seen incorrect in this context, but it is not, if by race we mean (quoting the dictionary verbatim): "the sharing of characteristics, whether morphological, genetic, ecological or physiological, which differ from those of other populations of the same species". All anyone need do is to apply the above definition to any meek person, to realize that it hits the nail on the head. They are certainly a race – the adjective "dangerous" follows of its own accord. Madame Georges Courrier was dangerous, without a shadow of a doubt.

At any rate, the meek old lady began to feel ill at the beginning of the winter of 1902, around November or December. The family's New Year celebrations were held at home, in an atmosphere already tinged with uncertainty about the future, for both the old and the new Madame Courrier.

The elder woman betrayed the occasional sign of weakness. For example, she proved unable to impose her choice of "boeuf à la mode" for New Year's Eve dinner; her daughter-in-law prevailed, with the novelty of roast duck.

"Never eaten such a thing in our house before," Alphonse's mother commented, concealing her resentment beneath a feigned docility, "but if it makes her happy . . ." She was having a heart-to-heart with her butcher, who, unable to provide his usual order of beef, had come round to deliver his season's greetings instead.

The younger woman, in her turn, betrayed her hopes of

future power, manifested on this occasion in the innocuous guise of the bird which had been sacrificed and stuffed by her skilled hands in one intense afternoon, immediately followed by a morning of roasting in the wood-oven. It has to be said that, during this crisis, the younger Madame Courrier had her husband's open support – open yet wary, both because Alphonse did not know how the duck would turn out, and because this was an epoch-making change and, as such, deserved to be approached with caution.

It snowed, naturally, on Christmas Eve, and again on the night of the 31st of December. Nature respects tradition – something which only caused more pain to old Madame Courrier, who was witnessing, under her own roof, man's betrayal of this same tradition. To make matters worse, the duck was exquisite and she was forced to see the pleasure in her son's eyes. It would have been easier to forgive him a sin of lust. She began to die then, and there was no going back.

For the village, the third year of the century seemed to start without a hitch. Everybody met up at New Year's Eve Mass (Christmas and New Year really did get the entire village into church) and the pastor was able to count his happily united, closely-packed flock. The organ rang out solemnly; to the regular worshippers the service felt long, and they exchanged looks of mutual sympathy and devout patience. To the occasional churchgoers it felt positively punitive, but they too acquiesced, as this was an annual levy to which they submitted with good grace. Between each note emitted by the mighty instrument, which wheezed like a fat man struggling up a hill, there was plenty of time to look around and examine the entire population of the village. Everyone was present, although not all were as they had been at the last New Year's Mass.

The previous year, for example, Agnès had sat between her mother-in-law and her husband, while he now sat between the two women, their prisoner or their guard. Uncharacteristically, Germaine's hair was brightened by a colourful ribbon – too colourful for church. The year before, she had worn her hair in a plait, fastened untidily with what appeared to be string. She was sitting almost at the front, under the eyes of the priest. Her own elusive gaze wandered through the darkness of the vaulted ceiling and, from time to time, turned to seize a glimpse of what was behind her.

The Courrier family were sitting two rows further back, and all that the three of them could see of Germaine was the gold-bronze mass of her hair, which was far from disagreeable. At the very back, on the left, forgotten by both God and man, sat a woman, bundled up in a threadbare old coat. She was ugly, but she had remarkably smooth, fresh skin, like that of a Sleeping Beauty who has just been woken by a kiss. But who had dared to kiss her? The splendid young Madame Courrier – perfection being unknown in this world, and envy universal – had glanced furtively at the woman and felt a twinge of annoyance, as she lightly stroked a few minuscule red veins on her own alabaster cheeks. Old Madame Courrier had noticed the same thing, and felt privately gratified. All this in a church that was far from well lit, and just as the priest was about to elevate the Host.

At this point in the service the congregation kneeled, or rather the women did. The men, without exception, remained standing, rocking slightly as they shifted their weight sheepishly from foot to foot. The vet from the village over the hill was, curiously enough, among them. The priest raised the Host. Heads bowed, faces hidden in their hands (just like Agnès saying her prayers in the evening, thought Alphonse), the women finally concentrated on the service – with the exception of those whose fingers instinctively crept apart to allow a view of their immediate surroundings.

The Mass ended with a blast of the organ so powerful that it made the regulars jump, and deafened the ears of the occasional visitors, who got the impression that the priest was trying to brand his message for the coming year indelibly into their memories.

The occasion also marked the start of Alphonse Courrier's thirty-sixth year and, even at the sensible distance from which he viewed church affairs, he could not help thinking that the Te Deum which closed the year was somehow being sung in his honour. This was why he came: each 31st of December, he secretly celebrated the world before, and after, his arrival. This year's Te Deum had a special meaning for Alphonse: something along the lines of "The king is dead, Long live the king." Let this be said without malice: life is made up of such things.

Only the following day, the first of the year, as he sat in front of the aforementioned duck, did he begin to suspect it might actually have been a chorus of "Long live the Queen".

ELEVEN

"She's the best of women, really she is. My son couldn't have hoped for better. When my time comes" – here old Madame Courrier gave a deep sigh of Christian obedience – "I will go with a quiet mind."

Her hands were white, and could almost have been called well-tended; she delicately manipulated the white wool she was using to knit a pair of socks. Through the half-open door they could see the ever-so-slightly plump figure of her esteemed daughter-in-law, who was ironing in the kitchen. It must have been around the middle of January, and the elderly lady was talking to the butcher's wife, to whom she confided further examples of the protective tenderness she felt for the young Agnès.

"But . . . " she added finally, and that little word was all it took to rekindle a flame of interest in her confidante's bored eyes.

"But?" the latter prompted in a low voice, eager not to let the subject drop. There was a moment of silent suspense, followed by a cautious glance towards the kitchen, then, leaning precariously off her chair, the butcher's wife pushed the door noiselessly so that it almost closed, reducing their area of vision to a crack, through which they could see a corner of the table and a white table-cloth which moved along in little jerks, as if by magic.

"Did I say 'but'?"

The butcher's wife nodded vigorously. This was all she

needed: that this particular remark should get lost in the twists and turns of memory!

"You see, I really am quite happy," Madame Courrier said, "and I will die happy, although I have to admit, I'd have liked to have a grandson by now, to watch him grow up." Madame Chinot, the butcher's wife, relaxed slightly. She was afraid of missing something, because so far nothing really serious had come to light.

"There's plenty of time for that," she said. "I'm sure you'll have more than one to watch over, won't you?" The "won't you?" sounded as if it was carved out of her voice, half-way between a threat and a reassurance.

"Of course, I had Alphonse almost straight away," Madame Courrier went on. "The sooner the better, I'd have thought. Only God can afford to waste time. They're both in good health at the moment, but who knows what may happen? I haven't been feeling quite right myself lately. I feel as if something is missing. This house isn't the same for me any more, and . . ." Here came the crunch. Madame Chinot gathered her wits, and concentrated. She wasn't going to miss a syllable.

"Well, that's life. I dare say it's all for the best," Madame Courrier concluded with unwarranted haste, leaving her companion to ponder the vexation of everything she might have known. Madame Chinot returned to the attack, diplomatically.

"Of course it's all for the best," she said. "The Good Lord sees where man is blind. And in any case, what can you possibly be lacking? How on earth can your house have changed? Come now . . ."

Tears, or rather a suggestion of tears in old Madame Courrier's opaque eyes, appeared like a rocket in the night sky, illuminating Madame Chinot's horizon. She knew she could not – should not – press further. The only strategy in such situations is complete silence with, at most, a hint of a sigh to imply that such deep sorrow can only be respected, and that speech would be inadequate. All the more so as it would be far from easy to find the right words! Words which wouldn't ruin everything by stumbling through a minefield; words which wouldn't be asking. It is imperative not to ask. Any hint of curiosity would be fatal. Madame Chinot performed very creditably; the tension brought her to the edge of tears, which was going far beyond the call of duty.

Not even old Madame Courrier expected tears. She reached out a bony hand towards her neighbour's clenched fist, tapped her knuckles gently, and said:

"That's enough! Let's not talk about it any more. I'd hate to sadden you with my problems." She was struggling to convert her grimace into a smile. "Let's not talk about it any more."

Madame Chinot felt a rush of profound joy. Now she knew that next time − tomorrow, or even in an hour, if this visit lasted long enough − she would find out everything there was to know about the Courrier threesome. Unless, she thought gleefully, the threesome had not already become a foursome . . .

TWELVE

Except that Old Madame Courrier played her joker, and died that very night. Words cannot convey the depth of Madame Chinot's disappointment, but it is easy enough to imagine in any case. Darkness closed in on her: a darkness that was rendered more profound by the blinding ray of light which had preceded it. She heard of the death that same morning, as soon as her husband opened his shop; the first customers spread the news like salt on a wound.

She hastened, nevertheless, to the dead woman's house, running as fast as her legs would carry her, as if driven by the hope that Madame Courrier's face might retain some trace of what she had left to say – a half-word which had risen to her lips, and become entangled in the surrounding network of wrinkles or in her still-open eyes. But she was too late: the old lady's eyes were resting under their lowered lids, and her face had the enigmatic tranquillity of a mummy's. Everybody was touched by Madame Chinot's devotion.

Next to the body stood Alphonse and his wife, the latter a perfect picture of mourning: her clothes and face just so; a somewhat evasive gaze (but then again, Agnès never did look people straight in the eye); hands clasped just beneath her belt. Since she was blonde, and her skin diaphanous, black suited her better than her wedding dress had done. Alphonse, on the other hand, looked mildly ill-at-ease: he was missing his cigar, and he had not had a good night. In the pauses between accepting condolences, he was running through that night in his mind.

Nobody could describe his mother's departure as discreet. This did not surprise Alphonse in the least. He knew her well, beyond that veil of meekness in which the whole village believed. On that night Madame Courrier let it be known, in no uncertain terms, that her departure was going to be memorable. It is probable that, in her heart of hearts, the old lady was disappointed not to be surrounded by a flock of children and grandchildren to bless and caution before taking her leave (she'd been complaining about precisely that to Madame Chinot).

So, having roused husband and wife in the middle of the night with her hoarse wheezing, she fixed her eyes on her son and seized hold of his hands. It was at this point that Alphonse began to feel embarrassed: he did not usually touch his mother, or she him. He prized her fingers away gently, one at a time, intending to pass her over to Agnès while he went to look for a doctor. But his mother clawed at him again, tenaciously. She made him understand that she wanted to be propped up on pillows to ease her breathing, and indicated with a peremptory gesture that Agnès should fetch them. Her eyes followed the young woman out of the room, then she pulled her son down towards her, very close.

"She's got fatter, your wife," she said, before a lump of catarrh stifled her voice in her throat. When Agnès returned with the pillows, Madame Georges Courrier was already dead.

"I'll go and put these back," said the only remaining Madame Courrier. "I don't think we need them any more." She turned on her slippered heels, making the folds of her heavy night-gown swirl around her, and left the room.

Had she put on weight? Hard to tell without a dress to define her figure, but an element of grandeur about the waist was discernible beneath the softness of the flanelette. Alphonse watched her go out, then turned to his mother for one final consultation. She was still staring at him, with wide-open, glassy eyes. Even if Agnès had put on weight, what might be the cause? The so-called "letting go" of married life? Or that other, more private reason, which is usually hinted at for a while, without being openly proclaimed? If the latter, Courrier's mental calculations didn't add up. He removed his glasses and polished them on his vest, then slipped them back on and, just as mechanically, shut the eyes of the dead woman at his side.

Agnès came back into the room fully dressed. Alphonse shot her a questioning look.

"The priest, Alphonse. You have to go and call him," she said calmly – she had already prepared herself to receive the cleric.

"At this hour? And what's the use now anyway?"

"That's how these things are done, Alphonse. I've laid your suit out on the bed."

It was true that Alphonse was unpractised in the matter of funerals, while his wife knew the ropes, as only women seem to do on such occasions. He got dressed, wondering whether to hurry or take his time. In the long bedroom mirror he peered closely at his face, breaking it up into its constituent parts to see where he might resemble his mother. Two symmetrical creases at the corners of his mouth were identical to those of the dead woman, as was his way of pressing his lips together and delicately biting the tip of his tongue. He moved nearer to the mirror and touched the deep furrows at either side of his mouth. Time would draw out that similarity; for the moment, only he could see it.

Ten minutes later he was knocking on the priest's front door; five minutes after that, he was listening to the old man's gentle reprimand for not having called him sooner. The cleric was equipped with the tools of benediction, and from time to time he sighed, mourning the loss both of his sleep, and his elderly parishioner.

"*Tempus fugit*," he said, and the phrase seemed to suit both his losses equally.

They were greeted by a sorrowful Agnès, who was ready to play her part, which included preparing the deceased for burial – a process which had to be performed immediately, and required assistance. Alphonse was automatically exempt. Who, then?

"Germaine," Agnès said firmly. She lived just across the way, after all; if it hadn't been for the fact that, in winter, everybody kept their shutters closed, it would have been enough to lean out of the window and give her a shout. Germaine and her mother were the right ones.

"Wouldn't her mother be enough?" Alphonse asked. His wife shot him a rapier look.

"It'll be easier with three," she said – and she was right, of course. How would Germaine look after being woken in the middle of the night to perform such a task?

Germaine leapt at the chance to enter Monsieur Courrier's house, and to help on such a solemn occasion. He personally waited for mother and daughter at their front door and escorted them across the alley to his own house. In the dark, the young girl's hair shone as it had that other time, on Christmas Eve. In the dim light of the entrance hall, Alphonse caught her glancing at him, furtively. She was probably a little nervous; it seemed only natural to squeeze her arm as he directed her to the right room. This had the same effect as touching Mother Earth had on the giant Briareus: Germaine was filled with unexpected energy and handled the dead body with the ease of a professional. Agnès was impressed. And to think she'd never believed her to be worth a sou!

As for Monsieur Courrier, sitting in the kitchen: he finally lit a cigar and erased from his mind the ritual being performed next door, concentrating instead on matters within his area of competence. No shop the following day, then that sort of barely muted party which constitutes a funeral; voices in the cortege; handshakes. He could remember nothing of his father's funeral, yet now, wholly unprepared, he was going to have to play the leading role. But in this he was mistaken or, at least, he underestimated his wife – a common error among men.

THIRTEEN

The funeral took place three days later. For the second time in his life (the third, if we count his christening, but then he was only really playing a supporting role to his mother), Alphonse Courrier was entering the village church as main protagonist. Or so he thought. The days of the funeral vigil, with that discomforting presence in the house and all those people coming and going, had left him feeling greatly distracted. He had no deep sorrow to contain but, ever since the first morning, as he received Germaine's heartfelt condolences (she had shyly retained his hand between hers, without looking up), he had felt a shiver of – was it fear? No, not fear exactly: it was something less explicit, a slightly perverse insinuation, which sidled up to him and settled at his side, calm as you please. He could choose to ignore it, but there it was in any case. The feeling had arrived as he walked into his mother's room to see the results of the women's work. There she lay in the black dress she kept for best, and the shoes she never wore (they'd had some trouble getting them on) – all that useless paraphernalia which nobody would ever see again once the coffin had been nailed down.

His mind naturally went back to his night conversation with the vet that summer, and consequently to the vet himself, with whom he had been playing cards more often of late, so much so that they even occasionally had a game at Courrier's house. He stroked his beard and ran his thumb along one of the furrows beside his mouth: a barely perceptible legacy of his mother, who, now, in this place, was passing him another baton: the next in the family relay would be him.

By nine in the morning, the house was ready to receive visitors. The first, as we've already said, was Madame Chinot; after her there was a ceaseless coming and going. Death in the family is exhausting, but Agnès was perfect: she had a kind word for everyone, sweet wine on the table, and – conjured from who knows where – biscuits to be offered to all female visitors above a certain rank. It is not always apparent, in normal times, how vast the social structure of a village is, but funerals reveal it more than any other occasion.

The vigil lasted three days: an endless alternation of prayer and small talk in which Courrier had to participate, sinking, hour after hour, into the exclusively female world which was streaming through his house. The men sent their wives to pass on their condolences and Alphonse, shopless and duty-bound to remain at his post next to Agnès, experienced the odd moment of claustrophobia. His only distraction was dealing with the technicalities of the ceremony itself or, more precisely, with its cost, because naturally Agnès was dealing with the practical details. She made sure that everything was perfect; if it had been her own mother that had died, she couldn't have done more. Actually, if it had been her mother, she wouldn't have done anything of the kind: her behaviour here was related to something which Courrier gradually identified over the three days of the vigil.

His wife was behaving with an ease, a naturalness which could only be envied and admired. When – in an early afternoon break from visitors, just after the kitchen table had been cleared of lunch – Alphonse heard, or thought he heard, his wife humming a tune (a melancholy tune, to be sure, but a tune nevertheless), he lost all doubt that, not only was Agnès feeling no sorrow (which was fair enough), but she was actually brimming with a quiet joy. Women like her do not go in for loud outbursts or extreme shows of emotion. They manage their internal lives as they would the Marquis of Jocelyn's castle, if asked to: in an ordered and efficient manner. They polish their minds like the family silver. Now that the power was passing into her hands, Madame Alphonse Courrier was preparing herself with moderation and discipline for her forthcoming enthronement.

This took place in church, during the funeral service she had organised with such proficiency. Where she had got hold of the heavy black macramé veil she was wearing in the style of a Spanish mantilla, nobody knew. To tell the truth she would have preferred a hat – with a touch of fur on it perhaps – but that would have meant an incursion into foreign territory, so to speak. Hats were the prerogative of the (duly present) village aristocracy, and Agnès had a strong sense of what was fitting. The veil was perfect. At the sight of her sitting there with such aplomb, Madame Chinot, two rows behind, remembered the tears which, for a brief moment, had reddened her poor old friend's eyes. Why, she asked herself, hadn't she seized her chance to pluck the secret which was ripe for disclosure?

A coffin that eschewed both opulence and inadequacy dominated the centre of the nave. The Courriers, dressed in black, neither grief-stricken nor sombre, a picture of dignified composure, were alone in the front pew – usually reserved for the local aristocracy, but today given over to the leading players. There was a carriage and pair waiting outside the church upon a magnificent carpet of snow, which contrasted harmoniously with its funeral livery. The second pew from the front was occupied by Agnès' parents and the veterinary surgeon; behind them, seated in row after row, was the whole village. It was just like Christmas all over again.

Right at the back – alone, as she had been at Christmas – sat the woman in the threadbare coat. Courrier, turning round for a moment, recognised her, and felt an agreeable warm rush of blood to his head. He sighed deeply, pushed his glasses up a fraction and rubbed his eyes slowly, until he started to see double – a trick he used to play as a child. To his right, the curves of Agnès Courrier suddenly became doubly abundant. His mother had been right, Alphonse decided: Agnès had developed an imposing – but pointless – figure.

He remembered – inside that threadbare coat of a nondescript hue, beneath a dress that would certainly be just as shabby – a body, both muscular and docile; a body in which not a single cell was without vibrancy and life. A smile escaped him, at the memory of their blissful evenings in the hayloft, and he caught an approving look in his direction from the priest, who was extolling the virtue of confronting misfortune with serene Christian resignation. Suddenly he felt good, better than he had felt for a long time – and not by chance, he reflected, but right here, on this occasion. After all, mothers love their sons above all else, and this felt like a mother's farewell gift. Mother and daughter-in-law never had got on in any case. Madame Chinot would have had cause to rejoice.

FOURTEEN

The village had acquired a new milestone. Where people used to say "before Courrier opened his shop" or "Courrier's shop was already open, when my father –" etc, now they said "Can you remember if it was before or after poor Madame Georges Courrier's funeral?"

This communal watershed turned out, in a private, closed way, to be particularly meaningful for Alphonse.

On the day after the funeral, and its subsequent dinner for a select few, the shop re-opened its shutters. Alphonse wore a small mourning button on the lapel of his black overalls. It was hardly visible, and then only from very close up. It was against that button that the ugly Adèle's smooth cheek was firmly pressed by an ardent kiss, when she came in to buy a handful of nails for the carpenter's shop run by the men in her family. It was the first time she had been back to her old lover's den. (Old! Only a few years had passed, and middle-age suited them both.) She had not been expecting such an explicit welcome. It was not like him – or perhaps it hadn't been like him before his marriage.

Reunited at last with a soothing cigar; back in the shop, and aware that this territory at least was his and his alone; seeing her appear before him, as the dim light of dawn was still struggling to turn night into day, Alphonse had felt the same upheaval of mind and body which she had precipitated on the day of the funeral. This time he decided that there had been enough caution and, as he kissed her, he surrendered himself to a tenderness which promised not to end there. Then he regained his composure, put her money in the till and bade her goodbye as he would any other customer. Fortune favours the bold. At that very moment, his second client of the day came in, just late enough for a conspiratorial glance between man and woman to go no further than the four walls of the shop.

"Life goes on, eh, Alphonse?" the new arrival said in a tone of mournful consolation. "To think that only a month ago she looked in perfect health!"

I don't know if Alphonse had ever heard of LaPalice and his self-evident truths. In any case, he assented flatly, inhaled on his cigar so that the end glowed red, and went on looking patiently at his customer.

"Ah yes," said the latter, "I wanted some files – to keep on the cart in case anything went wrong with the horse's shoes." He was the last person who attempted to console Courrier.

And yet Alphonse had, in his own way, felt some sorrow: not excessive, not heart-breaking, but sorrow nonetheless. Sorrow, perhaps, at the fact that our common mortality is confirmed every time a living being dies. Also, to be more specific, he did not greatly relish returning home to a tête-à-tête with his wife. But he would have cut off his little finger rather than breathe a word about this to anybody. As far as the village was concerned, Alphonse Courrier was the man who had made the perfect match.

"In any case, they don't have children," Madame Chinot was saying to the tailor's wife. "Which means they can't. If every-thing was going as it should, you'd think that three years of marriage would produce some results. Can't I offer you a little currant syrup? Are you sure? I feel like a terrible hostess; you must be dying of thirst."

Madame Chinot's was the most thankless of tasks: weaving

the feeble threads of the story she had to hand, and somehow or other advancing her work. To this end, she was recruiting collaborators. She proceeded by instilling, in the minds of various women, a drop of suspicion that would poison first their peace of mind, then circulate freely through the veins and arteries of the village. Somehow or other she'd find a way to reach the heart of the matter.

"But they make such a lovely couple," said the tailor's wife. "They seem so happy. Even from across the road – you know, from Germaine's window – even from there, they never hear a voice raised in anger; never a quarrel, never a disagreement."

"That's just it!" Madame Chinot exclaimed. "That's what's odd about them. Every family has a row now and then. Take my husband: he's the most affectionate man on earth – and I say that after years of marriage – but even he has his moments, and I'm always the first to know: you should hear him yell! But that doesn't stop us having three healthy children, and that chapter's not necessarily closed, either." This was a bold assertion – a measure of Madame Chinot's frustration at her impasse over the Courrier puzzle. In any case, she decided, Germaine was worth cultivating, if only for being so close to the front line.

Germaine could have given her an answer, but she trusted nobody, least of all herself, so she guarded her thoughts jealously, more from fear of being proved wrong by the facts (which must be visible to others and not to her), than out of any superior sense of reserve.

Still, she had her answer: Alphonse Courrier was in love with her. The afternoon of the storm had left her with a suspicion, which a succession of small signs, unremarkable in themselves, had been enough to confirm. Nobody in a normal frame of mind would have timed Courrier's smile on meeting Germaine, or concluded that, if he slowed his pace as he approached his front door, it was because he was hoping she would appear on her own doorstep. As for the silence from the Courrier windows (mostly tight shut in winter), it was a sign of the melancholy which tarnished the family hearth. Happy couple, my foot! To think how short a journey – hardly more than a jump, three yards of alleyway – would have been needed, for her to be inside their house, unravelling the problem!

It was at this moment that Agnès asked her neighbour to help her out, twice a week, with the heavier housework.

It sometimes happens that Fate suddenly and unexpectedly grants us a wish but, in her rush to make us happy, she misjudges her aim by a fraction, so that we get what we wanted, but in a slightly altered form. Germaine longed to be inside Alphonse Courrier's house, but it was hardly ideal to come in through the tradesman's entrance. Nevertheless, she seized fortune, as it were, by the forelock, and was left with a tuft of it in her hand.

"Why ask Germaine, when you told me she couldn't do housework?" Alphonse asked curiously, when his wife informed him of the arrangement, which had already been finalised.

Agnès, who was bending over the sink to wash the vegetables for lunch, turned briefly to look at him. She was wearing a white apron with ribbons that crossed behind her back; it was spotless. She had the knack of not splashing herself even when washing salad. She could cook the most complicated of roasts without getting a single grease-stain on her clothes, and she wore an apron – embroidered, naturally – only out of vanity and self-discipline. The ones she chose were so refined and intricately made that . . . But Alphonse decided not to encroach on a subject which lay outside his domain.

As I was saying, Agnès turned to look at Alphonse.

"She won't be doing anything demanding," she said with a mildly ironic smile, "and nothing at all without my supervision.

She did a very good job when we dressed your mother. She seems to like our house: she was looking quite emotional – practically stroking the furniture."

"So? What's that got to do with anything? My mother's death must have upset her: she knew her quite well. And what she was doing wasn't easy. She's hardly more than a child, poor thing."

"Why 'poor'? She wasn't particularly fond of your mother."

"She was dressing a dead woman. I don't imagine that's something young girls do every day . . ."

Alphonse puffed irritably on his cigar, which went out. He got up crossly to look for a match and started rummaging about beneath the hood of the stove – a novelty that had been added to his mother's kitchen as a gift to the bride.

"The matches are on the dresser," said Agnès, without turning round.

"And when is she starting?"

"Next week; she'll be doing Mondays and Thursdays. She wasn't upset by your mother's death; something else is making her emotional."

"Do you know if she's set her heart on anyone? That kind of thing can have a strange effect you know, even on unrelated matters –"

"She's set her heart on you, Alphonse."

Agnès was leaning over the sink; Alphonse was leaning over the dresser, looking for the matches. They remained like that, their backs to each other.

FIFTEEN

In some people a taste for candour goes hand in hand with an intent to cause pain. Such candour will strike at a friendship like a bolt from the blue, cutting it short, but in fact it is always the result of a long-standing grudge. Over the years, Courrier had made a study of this (by no means secondary) element in the behaviour of his fellow-men. Not that he necessarily thought it an error to tell the truth, just that it could be incautious, to put it mildly. Like the thinking man and the observer that he was, he had accumulated a wealth of information on this subject, filing away in his mind each example he encountered, including exceptions to the rule, deviations and behavioural anomalies, until he eventually built up a picture which was almost definitive. At the very most he might have been missing some small piece of the puzzle, some slight nuance.

He himself preferred general truths: Truth in the philosophical sense of the word; digressions around the subject. On reflection, in everyday speech this word was ubiquitous, and was always given an absolute value. Courrier, as we know, had learnt to go easy on certainties. The presumption of certainty restricts one's defensive options; it allows more scope for being taken by surprise. And Courrier disliked surprises, good or bad. He used the phrase "it's true" as little as possible, and found it rather annoying in others. For most people the expression was not much more than an empty cliché. It entered a child's vocabulary disconcertingly early, and persisted into adulthood with an equally worrying tenacity.

It was not that Courrier was any less confident in his opinions than the next man – quite the opposite. Possibly he wouldn't allow himself the luxury of the word "truth" simply in self-defence, or because he wanted to be seen to be consistent. Expressions like "To tell the truth", or "If the truth be told" began so many sentences. It reminded him of the evangelical "Verily I say unto you", which to Courrier sounded damnably binding. For him to utter such statements, the world on the other side of his gold-rimmed lenses would have had to acquire an unchallengeable clarity – magnified, so to speak, by the clarity of the lenses themselves, which Courrier polished meticulously every morning.

But even when he trusted his own judgment implicitly, he did not trust others as repositories of the truth. Among the many who tried to foist on him a "truth" that was already as worn as his shop overalls, he had learnt to distinguish between those who were in bad faith; those who were making a rough estimate; the credulous, who were transmitting the unverified truths of others – and the curious, who were fishing for information by casting a few supposed truths as bait. Each of these categories was unreliable and inconstant in its opinions. All, that is, except his wife. When Agnès Courrier, née Duval, told you something was true, it was true. Because she – the missing piece in the jigsaw – used the truth with the assurance and accuracy of a marksman. No other weapon was so well suited to her intent to wound. That was why Courrier – leaning over the dresser, match in hand – could not help feeling for his wife the sort of admiration you feel for those who have honourably beaten you in a contest.

SIXTEEN

Never in her most ambitious dreams had Madame Chinot dared hope for such precious assistance in her research. Germaine, already her chief observer on the ground, was about to penetrate the territory under investigation, as her unwitting spy. She discovered this from Germaine's mother one morning, when the old lady was visiting the Chinots' butcher's shop requesting something to make broth with. She meant bones, of course – meat was for the rich. Anne-Marie Chinot was helping out in the shop when the girl's mother told her the news, with a melancholy sigh. Germaine could aspire to something more refined, such as serving at table or seeing to the cooking from time to time. Heavy housework wasn't exactly ideal. She sighed again, raising her eyes to heaven.

"Still, it'll be good experience for the girl," she said, to console herself. "To run a household properly you have to know how to do everything, and when it's her turn to get married . . ."

"Has she got anyone in mind yet?" inquired Madame Chinot, concerned that she might not have time to prepare the ground. She was not especially quick-witted, Germaine. To get anything out of her you had to resort to patience and slow training.

"She's still young – " her mother said.

"Oh yes, much too young. So when is she starting work?"

In a few days time! Fate is never gratuitously cruel, Madame Chinot thought to herself, and twice a week was not to be scorned as an opportunity to interpret any clues a household might let drop.

"About the bones," Madame Chinot said. "Next time, don't trouble to come for them yourself. Send your daughter. She may come for the Courriers' meat anyway. Madame Courrier, the young lady, she's the only one left now." A touch of gentleness had entered her voice. "And I don't think she likes shopping much. She almost never comes to us, anyway. Of course my husband knows their order, and he delivers it to their house, out of friendship for Monsieur Alphonse. But then, since old Madame Courrier died (Old! What am I saying? she was only – not even sixty), everything has changed in that house. Even their eating habits. She'll notice that, your Germaine. I wouldn't be surprised if they'd rearranged the furniture. Of course I can't say for sure. I haven't set foot in the house since the funeral."

This, for anyone with the sense to hear what was being said and the will to act, was as good as a formal commission, and Germaine's mother was precisely the sort of woman who could grasp the mission at once, and judge its possible risks and rewards.

Germaine, on the other hand, grasped only that she would be permitted, twice weekly, to enter her idol's temple. In truth she sensed that the best place would have been the shop, because there he really was lord and master. He spent less of his time at home, where the power lay in other hands. But it was a step in the right direction. Who could say whether, at some time in the future, they might not need someone to help tidy the shop after work, once the wooden shutters were closed and all the customers had gone? Germaine's head was reeling with excitement at the prospect, but she was a timid soul, and such a proposal, issued immediately, would have frightened her. Rather she was counting on the slow advance of time. Step by step, move by move, she would reach her apotheosis: Alphonse Courrier's hand stroking her hair; his voice behind her murmuring: "So very wet, my little one . . ." Her imagination was incapable of making him say anything more; she had become stuck at that point.

She started her new job on a Monday, when Alphonse Courrier had already gone out, leaving the smell of cigar-smoke in his wake. Germaine sniffed it calmly; she had the whole morning ahead of her. On that first day her task was to help the mistress of the house turn over the mattress and take the sheets out to the village wash-place. She entered the bedroom with some trepidation, understandable on at least two counts: it was her first job, and this was Monsieur Courrier's bed. Of course the idea that Madame Courrier also slept there troubled her, but only for a moment. However inexperienced Germaine might have been, for some strange reason she did not fear her rival in the least; on the contrary she sensed that she herself was the one to inspire fear. She worked hard, with an ease which, in the best of circumstances, Agnès would have expected only after months of experience.

The walk across the alley, the mistress of the house thought to herself, must have been bracing for the girl.

Thursday was the day for the floors. These – including the red-tiled kitchen floor – had to be polished until you could see your reflection in them. Her mistress was busy cooking something special for that evening. They must have been expecting a guest to dinner, but no information of any kind was forthcoming.

At the end of her first week, Germaine had not once had the joy of seeing Monsieur Courrier, or at least had seen him no more than she used to, by spying on his homecoming from her window. She was right about the dinner, and the guest turned out to be Alphonse's card-playing friend, the vet. Germaine waited all day with bated breath to be asked to help – at least

74

to wash the dishes, if not to wait at table. But no word came. Then, at around eleven in the evening, she saw the two men step out of the house into the dim light of the alleyway. It was the middle of February and the evenings were very cold. She watched them set off side by side, all wrapped up against the cold, and managed – by craning her neck to peer through the slats in the shutters – to follow them until they were swallowed up by the bend in the alley. She imagined that Courrier must be accompanying his friend part of the way home, so she remained at her post, barefoot on the cold floor, awaiting his return.

The church bells rang out three o'clock in the icy morning when Alphonse reappeared at the end of the alley, calmly unlocked his front door, struck a match to light his way in the pitch-dark house, and shut the door behind him. Not even the faithful Germaine had managed to keep watch so late.

SEVENTEEN

This is not so much a chapter as a review of the facts, for the benefit of those who, at the end of the previous page, may have felt tempted to draw certain conclusions; those who thought they could read something of significance into so late a home-coming.

After leaving the house at eleven, Alphonse Courrier and the vet had gone to the hardware shop, where Alphonse kept his ledgers. He needed some advice on money he was owed by a client he mistrusted, and he needed to check the dates and the figures. That was all. The two men discussed the matter, then Courrier put the book back in its drawer, and they continued to chat peacefully by the hot stove. That is an exact account of events on that Thursday night. The fact that this chance visit to the shop set a useful precedent was, I think, entirely accidental. Unless, that is, we choose to attribute to a man's brain such a capacity for unwitting subconscious actions, such duplicity and skill, that it can circumvent, even before the obstacle of his will, that of the conscious mind itself.

Be that as it may, as Courrier made his way home at three o'clock on what was now Friday morning, it occurred to him that the whole process might easily be repeated, so long as he took care not to disturb his wife, who might well be woken by noises in the night, or by the light of his lamp.

From that time on, Courrier went back to the shop after dinner fairly often – sometimes alone, sometimes accompanied by the vet, after one of their convivial evenings, which became more and more frequent. On those nights when he was there on his own, as he sat working by lamplight, he even caught himself wishing for some dramatic nocturnal event, such as a fire, or someone being taken ill. Such a crisis would have allowed his fellow villagers to find him wide awake – and alone – in his shop, so that it would be on record that this habit of his was entirely professional.

By Easter (which fell very early that year) Courrier's late nights had become routine. His wife raised no objections, nor was the rest of the village surprised. On the contrary, Madame Chinot and her allies were almost grateful to him: they took this to be confirmation of the unsteady marriage they had been speculating about for some time.

It was around the beginning of May that Adèle first slipped furtively into the shop, through the back door.

EIGHTEEN

The period from May to Christmas passed in an instant. Courrier had reached the age when every season pursues the next as closely as dogs sniffing each other's hindquarters. The stuffed duck reappeared, and the table was once again laid for three: the vet lived alone, so it seemed natural to invite him to join them for Christmas Day, particularly after their recent bereavement. A year – or slightly less – is not a long period of mourning for a village, and Alphonse still wore the black button on his jacket.

On this occasion Agnès, inspired by the presence of a guest, gave her all in the kitchen. To tell the truth, the vet had become an established presence in the house and could hardly be classed as a guest, but this festivity engendered a truly memorable lunch. One might almost think that Agnès had been researching the various courses for months – that she had gone so far as to carry out secret trials of the possible combinations. Germaine's household may well have known something about this, since, after work on Mondays and Thursdays, the girl would occasionally leave the house carrying a mysterious parcel or basket, perhaps containing the fruits of some experiment that had not attained the perfection the mistress of the house was aspiring to – though it probably wasn't far off.

Her determination was such that she did not even seek her husband's opinion during these intermediate stages. She preferred the deferential neutrality she got from Germaine and her mother, to whom these dishes, which she still considered perfectible, must have seemed like the veriest delicacies. It should be explained, by the way, that the standard of living in the Courrier household had reached quite a high level; that was the reason for all this expenditure on food (which abated considerably after the festive season).

And what of Madame Chinot? Had she no comment to make from her observation post? The fact is that the butcher's wife was suffering from an acute shortage of information. Her husband continued to supply the Courriers with their usual order, so there was no irregularity to register in that department. As for her extra supplies, Madame Courrier, in an unforeseeable gambit, had learned to drive the gig, so that she could go shopping elsewhere. Her family's village, only a few miles from the one she now lived in, was a dependable source of provisions. In the winter, when the snow made its punctual appearance, Agnès overcame the conditions by seeking help from her guest, who was only too eager to increase his standing in the eyes of the beautiful mistress of the house. When Christmas dinner finally came around, the only person to be really surprised was Alphonse.

But before we embark on that meal, we should record another fact of some note concerning Madame Chinot. The poor woman had been left standing, so to speak, with regard to the Courrier establishment. Her potential ally – that Germaine on whom her hopes had rested – far from being helpful, seemed quite incapable of observing her surroundings, let alone understanding them, and communicating her impressions. Tied to the Courrier house by an unwarranted loyalty – or by the utmost stupidity – she kept as silent as the grave. It was impossible to glean a thing about the work she did there, still less about her mistress' behaviour towards her. As for Alphonse's state of mind when he was at home – you might just as well have asked him: he'd have been more forthcoming.

"Germaine, go to Madame Chinot's to get us something for this Sunday. You know what we need," her mother had said, some time after her chat with the butcher's wife. But Germaine had refused. This was so unusual, that her mother thought she must have misheard the girl, and gave her a questioning look which implied that, if a "no" really had slipped out, there was still plenty of time to retract it.

"No," Germaine repeated, quite clearly. She went on to explain, tripping over her words somewhat, that she had a job now, and she couldn't be available in the way she had been. It was an important job too, one that would keep her out of the house more and more often, and not just for heavy housework. And going to Madame Chinot's was out of the question: the instinct which, where Germaine was concerned, deputised for intelligence, sensed an ambush. The girl's eyes were a pitiful sight, so affected were they by the effort of refusing, which seemed to be concentrating itself in them, dragging them into a frenzied dance as they strove to avoid the gaze of her mother (who, lucky woman, was in total control of her pupils).

"What's this about extra work?" the elder woman asked, interested suddenly, and placated.

Germaine swallowed hard.

"In the shop," she said.

"Monsieur Alphonse's shop?" asked her mother. "What would you be doing there? Don't tell me he wants you to be a shop-assistant! You don't know anything about hardware . . . Well?" she insisted.

"He wants me to do the cleaning, after the shop shuts."

This was the first her mother had heard of this, and she eyed her daughter curiously, watching for signs of deception.

"When did they ask you to start?"

"We haven't talked about it properly yet. I don't know when.

Perhaps from next month, when I'll have – "

"When you'll have what?"

"I meant when I'm a bit freer from the housework, from Madame Agnès. Then I'll go twice a week to help Monsieur Alphonse close up the shop."

When a person is cross-eyed it is hard to say whether they're avoiding your gaze intentionally. On this occasion, Germaine's defect was a considerable help in confusing her mother as to the truthfulness, or otherwise, of claims which her interrogator thought sounded far-fetched. The old woman would have sprinted across the alley there and then to ask Madame Courrier about it, if her daughter's conspiratorial air hadn't left her feeling unsure of herself, doubtful whether an untimely intervention might not jeopardise such an important decision – perhaps making them think she was trying to force their hand. That was the last thing she wanted. There could be a bright future awaiting Germaine: from cleaning lady to (in time, obviously) shop-assistant in the most flourishing concern in the village. This last mental leap had been made by the mother alone; it was not in her daughter's plans – those were set on quite another course, towards other dreams, which she had perhaps been too hasty in revealing.

It was Germaine's mother who went to buy the bones for their Sunday broth. She went to receive and impart information, uncertain to the last about her role in the game with the butcher's wife (who, in the absence of anyone better, was now lying in ambush for her).

Neither Alphonse nor his wife had ever entertained the idea which had taken complete hold of Germaine's mind. The news which the girl had given as true to her mother (and which she believed in herself) was an example of what is known as paranoid projection. We can even pinpoint the source of this paranoia (a solemn word for what, in this case, was simply a mildly overactive imagination): total lack of contact with Alphonse Courrier.

Months of work had turned that house into a place of thirst. Occasionally, as she scrubbed the kitchen floor, she might hear him come in the front door, walk along the corridor and go upstairs, without glancing round even for a moment, and always accompanied by the voice of his wife. It was quite clear: Madame Courrier did not want their eyes to meet, even for a fraction of a second, and was contriving to keep them apart. Now, Germaine could conceive of only one possible solution: Monsieur Alphonse had to ask her, straight out, to work for him. Faced with her husband's firmness of purpose, Madame Courrier would never dare to refuse, and what right would she have, anyway? It was all very simple. The only question she sometimes asked herself was how long it would be before he made the request, and why he hadn't already done so. Could he be afraid that she herself would refuse? Anticipating this eventuality, she had now come up with an indirect way of letting him know that she was ready to work in the Courrier shop.

Who knows whether Germaine was so very intelligent – from her point of view – as to devise the idea of using her mother to disseminate the story, or whether it was just that the flood of emotion built up during the tense days of waiting had so filled her heart that it spilled out in premature words?

Naturally Madame Chinot heard the news immediately. The subterranean but unerring route which the rumour then took, passed through almost every kitchen in the village, then crossed the local boundaries and, after a series of meanderings which would be hard to reconstruct, reached Alphonse's friend, the vet. That was how the news came to Alphonse himself, a couple of evenings before Christmas, in the shop, at a prudent distance from Agnès, and on a night when the coast had also been left clear, however reluctantly, by Adèle.

NINETEEN

"Who'd have thought it?" Alphonse said, removing the cigar from his mouth and rotating it between finger and thumb to inspect its glowing ash. To be absolutely honest his tone was that of a man who had been pleasantly surprised. Opposite him, the vet was toying with a screw on the table-top. He set it rolling and watched it loop round in an oval, then come to a stop, wobbling slightly.

"So? What do you intend to do about what the girl's been saying? – Unless somehow or other it was you who made her think such a thing."

"Not at all, my dear doctor. But I think it's an excellent idea."

The vet's mouth opened – whether to ask a question or to let out an exclamation, I couldn't say. In any case, it remained open, as if his jaw had locked. It took him a moment to recover the thread of the conversation, and he did so with caution, because it was one of those threads which cut into the hand if grasped too tightly.

"Where I come from, Alphonse, we call that playing with fire," he said.

"And where I come from, fire keeps you warm," said Alphonse.

It was two days before Christmas; outside, the ground was covered in snow; inside, the lamp gave off a yellowish halo of light and the stove in the corner burned hot. Alphonse felt perfectly at ease; the shop was his kingdom and the vet a passing traveller paying him homage. To each the government of his lands and the devotion of his subjects. Six hundred metres away, Agnès Courrier (née Duval) was governing her own with equal sagacity. Before too long, it would be her turn to receive due homage from the traveller.

Thirteen years later, on another night just before Christmas, Alphonse would recall, with perfect clarity, the words they spoke in the shop that evening.

In the meanwhile, once the festive season was over and the new year had reinstated the daily routine, Germaine had made the longed-for change of work – a total change, because she had been sacked by Madame Courrier and taken on by her husband. And nobody – except in the privacy of their homes; except among their very closest friends; except just between themselves and their confessor – nobody, I repeat, found anything objectionable in the arrangement.

TWENTY

At the age of thirty-seven Alphonse Courrier made his wife pregnant for the first time.

It was not by chance that Alphonse embarked late, and with reluctance, upon this chapter of his life. It proved to be the thorniest chapter, the most awkward. He fathered two sons because he felt obliged to. His sense of duty was not the result of Madame Chinot's insinuations, or even his mother's now long-distant hints. Fatherhood was part of his life-plan, which he had drawn up rationally and implemented just as rationally. He had deliberately chosen a wife of a certain solidity and attractiveness, precisely so that she would pass on good seed, and cultivate it responsibly. Children, Alphonse had theorised, should be the fruits of reason, because passion is almost always a poor counsellor. The passion which made him tremble with desire for the worst dressed, most ungainly woman in the village would, if left to itself, have led him, quite literally, down an ugly path. Adèle's unattractively close-set eyes and prominent cheek-bones would not have combined happily with Courrier's symmetrical face, his regular features, and the chestnut tones of her hair would have thrown a shadow over the gold of his beard. As for Adèle's voice, it was hoarse and expressionless. Or was that just because she was forced into a permanent whisper by their clandestine relationship? In moments of pleasure he had even been known to cover her mouth with his hand – once she had bitten him, gently, like a cat warning that it does not wish to be touched.

Anyway, if Alphonse had needed to think hard before having children, Agnès performed her duty perfectly. Their first child was male, and healthy. About a year later, the continuation of the family was bolstered by a second pregnancy, which resulted in another boy. And there the chapter of procreation ended. In its place another was opened: one dealing with education, but that too appeared likely to progress in an entirely natural way.

All of a sudden the storm which, only a year before, had been gathering around Courrier (or so Germaine – not without justification – had hoped, and the vet had feared), was dissipated in the pallor of Madame Courrier's breasts. During the long winter evenings, she nursed her sons with consummate ease, in front of their father and (why not, after all, given their intimacy?) the even more solicitous veterinarian, whose area of expertise, albeit restricted to the animal kingdom, conferred on him a physician's privileges.

"It was high time your husband gave you this jewel," the friend of the household observed, one of the first times he was permitted to watch their firstborn at dinner. Alphonse listened to him with a shudder of disgust. Lyricism dismayed him, whoever indulged in it; he feared it as a symptom of a pernicious weakness, akin to the emotional incontinence of children and the very old. Agnès, on the other hand, accepted the homage with suitable aplomb. She played her part to perfection: that of a queen filled with tender pride in her son, and rendered all the more beautiful by the gentleness of motherhood. Courrier was reminded of the story of Cornelia Gracchus, (a name he found unpleasant enough in itself); it was no coincidence that this parable of motherly love in ancient Rome made no great mention of the father.

A father (to return to our own story) who kept out of the way, observing the evolution of his species – that survival of the family name which seemed to be of such great importance.

The Courriers had secured another step towards immortality, represented at present by a kind of wrinkled monkey which, for the time being, did not evoke any particular emotion in its father. Newborn babies are essentially strangers who burst into the well-established lives of their parents, and win unmerited, yet universal, approval for the mere fact of having begun to exist. This creature which drummed with steady hand on Agnès' breast, displaying a familiarity which Alphonse Courrier had never allowed himself – not with his wife, at least – was irritatingly arrogant. The "jewel", as the vet referred to him, did not glitter in the least in his father's eyes.

As soon as the mother had recovered from the birth, a date had to be set for the christening. The child's name was not even debated: Agnès decreed he was to be Georges, after his paternal grandfather. Alphonse didn't think much of this backwards step. Georges had been his father's name, but since continuity was the issue here, he didn't see why names should recur every two generations. If his son ever had an heir, would he have to be called Alphonse – the name Germaine didn't like? Germaine who, from her corner, had been sorrowfully following Madame Courrier's triumphant pregnancy. When she came with her mother to visit the infant, she uttered a barely audible congratulation, which her mother augmented with a polite smile and an amazed glance at her daughter.

Alphonse was in the room during this visit, observing the scene out of the corner of his eye. He seemed harmless, even superfluous. Then, all of a sudden, he asked:

"Germaine, would you like to be godmother to my son?"

TWENTY-ONE

The Auvergne is a land of extinct volcanoes. Nowadays its fiery craters have become tranquil lakes, and the deep gloom of the pine forests which cover their shores seems unlikely ever to be pierced by flames again. No such eruption has recurred since the dawn of man. The Auvergne appears to be a peaceful land. But geologists know that spent volcanoes never entirely renounce their igneous nature; at most they might forget it for a while.

I couldn't say whether the composition of the rock, and the underground turmoil, act as a counterpoint to the nature of the people who walk that ground. Perhaps it is true that certain vibrations touch our psyche and that magnetic waves imperceptibly caress our minds.

Be that as it may, Courrier's alarming question about the christening could only have originated deep within the earth, and it had predictable seismic consequences. The Goddess of Motherhood dropped her mask for a moment; for a moment her features reorganised themselves into those of the harpy which Alphonse had so perceptively identified in her during their first days of marriage. A lioness defending her cub would have done no less, but animals are so much more elegant. Still, who can blame a young mother who, as she sits in adoration by the cradle of her firstborn son, hears his moral tutelage being nonchalantly assigned to the ex-charwoman? Agnès felt as if she were living a slightly modified version of the story of Sleeping Beauty, with cross-eyed Germaine in the role of the wicked witch, but this time invited to the christening – and how cordially!

Agnès placed little Georges in his cradle and tucked him in well, but the hands which fussed over his blankets and lace were, in reality, gathering up strength to crush the enemy at the outset. Anyone observing her closely would have spotted a barely controlled tremor. When she had finished, she drew herself up to her full height and bared her pink gums in a broad smile.

"I don't know who my husband wants to mock most: me, or your daughter," she said to Germaine's mother. "He can be a bit eccentric at times. But then, you all know him very well in the village, maybe better than I do. I'm sure you know him too, Germaine, don't you? Better than I do . . ."

Germaine's eyes had filled with tears. She could hardly see, but she managed to make out the blurred movement of a dark figure leaning against the dresser; she distinguished the red glow of his cigar and the glint of his glasses. He was approaching her, slowly, and she turned her wildly agitated eyes to him. The red dot at the centre of his mouth melted away, and his white teeth shone against the gold of his beard. He was about to say something to her; to her, like that time in the shop, during the thunderstorm – the time he had lifted his hand to touch her hair.

"I wasn't joking at all, Germaine," Courrier said. "You were called on to dress my mother for her funeral; it is only right that you should accompany her grandchild to the font."

Silence.

Had it ever occurred to Germaine to wonder what it would be like to die in a state of grace, plucked from the suffering of this earth to sit on a triumphal throne, she could never have imagined such a perfect apotheosis, or have choreographed it better. The other two women, on the contrary, were having a little trouble with their respective imaginations. When you do not inhabit a world of extravagant fantasy, coups de théâtre are merely embarrassing and, most importantly, very difficult to handle.

From a purely technical perspective, the curtain should come down at this point, leaving the actors frozen where they are. But in the real world, life goes on, and the stillness of surprise is always followed by motion. What happened next took no more than a second, as lightning is followed immediately by thunder: the action, then the sound, of Alphonse Courrier's blond cheek being slapped. Germaine's mother dragged her daughter away by an arm before the girl had the time to take it all in.

The couple were left with their baby as the only witness. He was not sleeping, just lying quietly in the cradle, staring into the distance; he couldn't possibly notice anything yet.

"How could you think such a thing? And say it! In front of everyone – in front of me!" Agnès began her sentence in a deep bass voice and ended it as a soprano – a surprising vocal range for such a brief remark. She was probably talking to drown out the echo of the slap she had dared to give her husband. A slap which, it could safely be predicted, would have terrible repercussions throughout the village. The thought occurred to her that she'd have done better to murder him than to feed such a substantial piece of gossip to every single inhabitant of this wretched, stifling place.

"It wasn't in front of everyone; it was in front of the one person who was supposed to accept or refuse," Alphonse replied. He seemed to have arranged for some alter ego to receive the slap for him: he was calm, reasonable and soft-spoken. He felt, who knows why, as if he had just successfully settled a score which had been outstanding for months and months.

"If Germaine accepts," he continued in the same quiet tone, "she will be the the child's godmother."

"My son's godmother?"

"Exactly. Your son's godmother."

"Have you any idea what people will say? To think that my family believed . . ."

"Agnès, everybody is going to have so much to say, today, and for many days to come, that we'll have earned ourselves the gratitude of a whole village."

Germaine said yes.

TWENTY-TWO

This cost her dear, poor girl. Given the circumstances, no detail could hope to pass unnoticed, and she in particular would be in the eye of the storm. Everybody – including most of Madame Courrier's native village – would be at the christening, and it wasn't going to be a restful ceremony. She began to worry about what to wear, especially since Agnès was bound to make the most of her advantages, while Germaine hadn't the faintest idea how to hold her own. If Alphonse had wanted to get involved, he would perhaps have advised her to avoid competing altogether, as she was bound to emerge defeated and ridiculous. But no man gives such advice to a woman and, if he did, most women wouldn't listen. Germaine, however, so admired the man who had got her into this mess, that one word from him would have been gospel to her. If Alphonse had suggested it, she would have turned up at the ceremony in her apron.

In the event it was Madame Courrier who summoned her, two days after the drama. She asked her to come alone and not to advertise their meeting.

"I believe you have accepted my husband's . . . proposal," began Madame Courrier, somewhat stiffly. She was harbouring one last tenuous hope: all alone and unprotected in her presence, the girl might still give way, overcome by the magnitude of the undertaking. Madame Courrier found herself praying under her breath, rather as an old woman might talk to herself.

"Yes," replied Germaine. It might be the last word she had

strength for all day, but nothing on earth was going to make her withdraw her consent.

"Good," Agnès said. "Good. In that case we'll have to make the best of it." From the depths of her soul, Agnès could feel herself rebelling against reality. Even her words came out reluctantly, and refused to be marshalled into sentences.

"Have you any idea what you're going to wear? Whatever you choose, make sure it isn't garish. It is a religious ceremony, after all." She could have been talking to a savage who was unversed in the customs of a Catholic country – not to a village girl who, however inexperienced, went to church regularly and had an excessively pious mother.

Germaine swallowed hard. "I've got a black dress," she said.

Agnès raised her eyes to the sky. Of course: her mourning outfit – the one which, after a certain age, every woman kept to hand to cover all eventualities. A village always produces such eventualities.

"I'll give you something of mine," she said hurriedly, and barely had time to be amazed by Germaine's reply:

"I don't think so, Madame. I'm taller than you."

This was true: taller, and slimmer, to be precise.

"If the black dress is all you have – I was hoping for something better for my son's godmother, but a black dress will be less bad than – Oh, wear what you like," she concluded, defeated.

As Germaine crossed the threshold on her way out of the Courrier home, Agnès was seized by the urge to strike her a blow from behind, and her hands tightened unconsciously around the long handle of an iron pan balanced on the draining board. This movement tipped dirty water from the pan on to her dress and, from the depths of her heart, she cursed Germaine for having been born.

The next time she saw her was the morning of the christening. Tradition required that the child's parents and godparents – the role of godfather having gone to Agnès' own father – should carry the baby out of the house and walk in procession to the church, accompanied by friends and relatives. These walks were solemn yet cheerful occasions, whatever the weather. It had been a while since the last christening procession in the village, and the general satisfaction at the wealth of gossip surrounding this one meant that it was awaited with more than usual eagerness. The rumours were various; the factions were several. All behind Agnès on the female side, (although not without a touch of satisfaction that this queen without a crown was at last going to feel the sting of two or three thorns on her forehead). The men, for the most part, expressed amusement: they sympathised with Alphonse, and behind his eccentric gesture they detected the intention to set the two women against each other – an art practised by the male sex from time to time, with varying degrees of skill. And since everyone knew Alphonse was clever (nobody could equal him at cards), lack of skill was obviously not going to be a problem.

So we come to the morning of the ceremony. It was a splendidly sunny day, of course: that beautiful October sun which sinks early behind the hills, but still warms you nicely, like a blanket over your shoulders. Almost all the close friends had gathered in front of the Courriers' house; the rest of the village would wait for them at the entrance to the church. The parlour was all laid out for the reception, to be followed by a lunch for twenty or so guests. Madame Courrier was weary from all the work which had gone into the day. She had received every possible assistance from her mother and sisters, but the responsibility remained hers alone, and she could not afford to have a teaspoon out of place. There had been times when she had felt so overwhelmed by the sheer volume of things to do, that, for a fraction of a second, she even forgot why she was organising this knees-up for twenty.

But, on the morning of the christening – which might as well have been afternoon for her, she got up so early – she was ready by nine o'clock on the dot, and she looked splendid. Her golden hair was kept in place by a myriad of pins, whose heads shone like pearls. She wore a dove-grey dress in the very best of taste. A real lady does not draw attention to herself with extremes of any kind: this was holy writ to Agnès Courrier. She was even wearing a little something on her head: a snippet of material which did not hide her hair, but feigned compliance with Mother Church's injunction to cover one's head. This was her only piece of daring – the only touch which exceeded the limits of discretion and the categorical imperative never to wear hats, because hats were for upper-class ladies.

She was universally admired, and the vet, who had entertained the hope of becoming godfather (and, as each day passed, had believed he saw clear presages of a request, which never materialised), became quite dewy-eyed. Only Germaine was missing, and the guests began to turn their attention to the house across the way, which showed no sign of life. Closed shutters and total silence. Then the front door opened and the old lady came out; behind her was Germaine.

She was wearing red. Where on earth had she got hold of that dress from the last century? It was tight-waisted, with flounces and a large bow at the back: straight out of the wardrobe of Empress Eugénie. Agnès Courrier opened her eyes wide and raised a hand to her mouth, presumably to stifle a cry. But nobody was paying any attention. Her dove grey was utterly eclipsed by the flame which lit the doorway with its hesitant flicker.

TWENTY-THREE

This is the story of a dress, as it was recounted by Alphonse to the vet, a little while later. It was deep winter by then, in 1905, and little Georges was a few months old. He was growing well, apparently unscathed by the singular circumstances of his christening.

"Just between ourselves, I don't think anyone could claim that, when the time came, Germaine wasn't up to the task," Courrier said. "What was wrong with her anyway?" he asked rhetorically, inhaling cigar smoke and savouring it deep in his lungs. Some people find this poison spreading through their bronchial tract into the whole of their chest as bracing as the highly oxygenated air on top of a mountain. If it is true that the mind has a role to play in keeping us physically well, that moment of pleasure must surely improve their health.

The two men were in the shop, late one afternoon. In fact it was closer to early evening: it was pitch dark outside, since the few gas lamps were smothered in snow. The vet had given up smoking, and consequently was observing Courrier with a certain envy.

"The dress," he replied.

"You mean the red dress?" asked Courrier. "Little Georges was christened in water and fire, my dear friend! There's not many can say that."

"It was such extraordinary behaviour! Who'd have thought it of such a modest girl?"

"Now don't tell me she didn't look good in it! Tell me frankly – didn't it suit her?"

"Why drag the whole thing up again, now that it's over?"

"Because I'd like to have an unbiased opinion – if you are unbiased –" (here Alphonse cast a sidelong glance at the vet) "on such a – well, on not so very trifling a matter."

The elderly vet sighed deeply. Of course it was not trifling. In this village, lost among the extinct volcanoes and buried beneath a hard winter's snow, Germaine's red flame flared up again for him with renewed intensity.

"Where on earth can that dress have come from?" the vet wondered, out loud.

"From my house."

Alphonse followed this reply with a good lungfull of restorative smoke.

"Alphonse! Are you serious?"

"It was my mother's. I don't think she ever wore it. It was too red for a woman of her temperament, too flashy. It's the same problem my wife has – the same as all women who are supposedly elegant, but not very daring. Their kind always produce good mothers, and magnificent housewives. If you meet one, you're lucky. I met one, dear doctor. I'm a lucky man. I have a wife who would never wear red."

"Anyway," he went on, "it was a wasted dress: hidden away in a drawer in my parent's room. I don't think anyone had taken it out for forty years. Agnès had certainly never seen it, and she'd never have dreamt it was there. Do you know where it came from?" He leant towards his friend in a confidential manner. "I bet you can't guess."

"You're right there," said the vet. "I can't." Then, in response to Alphonse's deliberately long pause, he asked: "Well? Where did it come from then?"

"From the Mont-Dore. The hotel with the thermal baths in

97

the centre of town. I wasn't even born, so it must have been around 1865, just after my parents got married."

"So your father used to give presents like that to his wife?"

"No, no, of course not. He'd never have done it of his own accord. It just happened."

The vet gave Alphonse a puzzled look, unsure as to whether to believe his story or not. To the country folk of the Auvergne, the Mont-Dore was the navel of the world, though they never went there. It was the navel of a different world: the world of the urban rich, of Parisians on holiday. It took money and panache to go there. Country folk might have had the former, but they had none of the latter.

"What was your father doing at the Mont-Dore?" the vet asked.

Alphonse drew on his cigar and absent-mindedly stroked the mourning button he still wore on the lapel of his black overalls.

"He didn't usually go there," he replied. "It happened by chance. You may remember that my father, among other things, used to act as a land agent. He needed to clinch a deal with some men from Lyons, and he wanted to do it discreetly, without being seen by anybody local. The meeting went well; everybody was pleased, and on top of his percentage, they paid for my father to stay a night at the Mont-Dore."

"So he thought he'd buy your mother a dress, as a souvenir," the vet deduced.

"How very unimaginative you are!" Alphonse almost said out loud. But he didn't like being impolite or sarcastic. People are as Nature makes them – better to appreciate their qualities than denigrate their shortcomings.

"He was the one who was left a souvenir, the following morning," he said. "It was lying in full view over a chair in his bedroom. She'd only left him her evening-gown!"

The vet was finding it harder and harder to follow. He

bowed his head slightly, to distance himself from the narrator.

"But why would she do that? What did she mean by it?"

"It may have been some form of compensation to my mother. Or a very clever way of driving herself between my father and his wife for ever. Who knows?"

"But who was she?"

"I haven't the slightest idea. All I've been told is that she was a woman with an extremely unattractive face. Does that surprise you? It's not so strange, believe you me: ugliness can have a special part to play in these affairs." He lowered his voice for no apparent reason. "It makes a woman more generous, for a start. After all, faces are just a fragment of the whole, but we insist on investing them with such tremendous importance. Or rather, the rest of you do – personally I don't value faces at all."

"What about your wife then?" the vet asked with a knowing laugh. "Why did you choose a beautiful one?"

Alphonse looked at him and returned the smile, but without a trace of irony.

"Because she was going to be a wife," he answered. He'd have bet his house that the vet hadn't understood! He looked at him more closely. "I said a wife, not my wife. Do you see the distinction? And she had to be a solid woman. Yes, solid – that seems to me the right word to describe my wife. Solid and irreproachable. I've never said this to anyone else, but you're my friend – I married her with the approval of a whole village. It wasn't easy, but it wasn't impossible, as you can see."

The vet couldn't decide which to believe in least: the improbable tale of the red dress left behind in a hotel room after a night of adultery, or the collective motive for a marriage. For the moment the story of the dress took precedence, particularly since there were still a few details missing.

"But how on earth does a man give his wife a dress that's

been worn by another woman? What – well, what kind of a nerve does that take? What excuse could one possibly use?"

"So you've never been to the Mont-Dore Hotel, I take it? All that's required is a well-aimed tip: to the wardrobe maid, in this instance. He got her to iron the dress and find one of those dressmaker's boxes. Then he folded it up and put it in. The dress looked brand new: it hadn't been worn more than two or three times."

"But to lay yourself open to the gossip of the hotel staff . . ."

"Hotel staff can find plenty to gossip about every time they change the towels in the morning. One more eccentric request means nothing to them. I suppose the story may have done the rounds of some other region of France; it depends where the maid came from. Who knows? Perhaps somebody in Brantôme knows the story of the red dress. Or in Poitiers, if you prefer."

"How do you come to know it in such detail?"

"There are some things a father tells his son."

"Really? I wouldn't have thought so. My father never told me anything like that."

The vet caught the ghost of a comment – unvoiced, of course – in Alphonse's eyes: to tell someone about something, you have to have experienced it.

"And what about you, what stories will you have to tell your Georges in a few years' time?"

Alphonse Courrier cast a moist-eyed look around the shop which, in the half-light, revealed to his expert eye every nook and cranny, warm as a bedroom alcove.

"I'll wait until my two sons are old enough, then I'll see."

"Two?"

"Precisely, Doctor. Two. In August."

TWENTY-FOUR

There would be no encore for Germaine. Her star never shone in the village sky again. Little Alain Courrier's christening saw her relegated to the background, a melancholy spectator at an event which had nothing to do with her. This time the leading roles went to Agnès' younger sister and the vet. The choice had again been made by Alphonse, in compliance with his wife's stated wish that he do nothing outlandish this time. She had made this request calmly, some time before the child was born, when certain whisperings led her to understand that the village, half in apprehension and half in pleasant anticipation of surprise, was expecting a second sensation.

And since Courrier greatly enjoyed surprising people, he concluded that his best option was to serve his fellow villagers a menu of flat normality. The uniformly grey procession wound its way more silently than the previous one, more sedately, and beneath duller skies. Germaine arrived in her black dress, lost among the second-class guests, at the back of the group. So much at the back, in fact, that she ended up next to the remote, silent, ugly woman who took part, with shadowy discretion, in every village function. The two of them exchanged a cursory greeting before each sank into her own thoughts. Germaine's were nostalgic and bitter with disillusion – it was written on her face. The face of the other woman was like a house with no windows: inside there could have been everything or nothing. Madame Chinot nodded at her briefly; not even she could muster any curiosity about so scrawny a creature, and one so free of secrets. She lived with her older brothers, who were carpenters. Sometimes she helped them out in the shop, when necessary even working as an unskilled labourer. By this time it had become obvious that she was not marriageable material. It wouldn't have occurred to any man to take her home as his lawfully wedded wife, and she, for her part, had never expressed any desire for a family of her own.

This Adèle had a reputation – if it can be called that – for being a loner. When she came into the village, she always seemed to be in a hurry; she never stopped to chat; she never wasted time. The daylight hours seemed priceless to her. The truth was that she was a night animal – or better, she was an animal with two natures. I hope I don't appear disrespectful with my insistence on the word "animal". It should be understood in terms of the fusion between a living creature and a creature possessed of a soul. Even Dante Alighieri says this.

Well, Adèle was a perfect whole, all the more so as she managed to hold her daytime and nocturnal natures together. Her physical body expressed itself during the day: in the effort of work; in her obstinate silence; in her mule-like obedience. Her soul took flight at night.

If ever a faithful woman has walked this earth, that woman was Adèle Joffre. Fidelity can sometimes be the result of a lack of imagination, of submission to convention, or simply of habit. Adèle's fidelity sprang from a love so pure it is almost embarrassing to discuss.

"Ugliness makes a woman generous," to quote Alphonse Courrier almost word for word: a remark made during the exchange of winter confidences with his friend the vet, who had been far from guessing what kind of comment he was hearing. He had assumed it to be theoretical, or something Alphonse's father had said, rather than a matter-of-fact statement. But Courrier was talking with all the authority of a man with intimate knowledge of his subject. Adèle had served as a kind of training-ground for the young Alphonse's sexual endeavours: an arrangement experienced by many boys, who soon move on and forget their first encounter. But in Alphonse's case something about that moving on had calcified his soul.

This was not visible from the outside. In the eyes of the world, Alphonse Courrier was a cheerful man, to whom Fate had dealt a good hand. Either side of his mouth he had deep creases, of the kind which sometimes develop in those who feign happiness. This probably results from the muscular effort of false laughter, which persists for longer than necessary and induces a deformity which closely resembles the mask of the Veio Apollo (for those who are acquainted with that sculpture).

Successfully camouflaged by his short beard, this tension remained a secret, and Courrier himself, noticing it in his face, would have been surprised at its being given such an interpretation. But when he happened to encounter Adèle's mouth again, he felt his features relax and smooth out. The Veio Apollo became the bronze Charioteer of Delphi.

He met her at night, for part of the night, twice a week. These rendezvous, regular as office hours, may sound unimaginative, but actually they were strangely comforting. Each one's life ran along well-established tracks; on Tuesdays and Fridays, this diversion slowed their speed, and allowed the two of them to alight and rest: in winter, in the quiet of the closed shop; in summer, still, occasionally in a hayloft (but with more circumspection, because haylofts are well-frequented places).

All stories have an inside and an outside. From the outside, had anybody known the details of Alphonse Courrier's life, they might well have thought him greedy. He had one official, relatively beautiful wife; two official, quite satisfactory sons and one minor bourgeois indulgence: secret transgression with a mistress. Add to this the fact that this mistress, unlike those in magazine romances, cost him nothing at all, and he could indeed be called a lucky man. But not a greedy one. In this particular instance, Alphonse Courrier's luck was of quite a different nature. Independent – like all real strokes of luck – from his own volition, it arose from one very simple truth: Adèle's body was compatible with his. Set against the great march of civilisation this sort of thing is of very little consequence, not to say irrelevant. But in the existence of one normal inhabitant of a village in the Auvergne (or any other region, come to that) it is of the utmost importance.

If Alphonse had realized all this earlier, would he have married Adèle? Certainly not. The compatibility of two bodies has nothing to do with registry offices, civil status, family estates . . . Such, at least, had been the firm opinion of the ironmonger at the time when he was building himself a solid, impregnable life.

Half-lying on blankets spread over the floor, one arm beneath Adèle's head, Alphonse narrowed his eyes.

"How long have I been married, Adèle?"

"Seven years."

He stroked her cheek. Her skin was as smooth as a baby's. Nowadays he could say that with full knowledge of the facts. Looking in from the outside again, two sons in seven years was not a bad score. Two sons born in the last two years. Two years, more or less, of regular encounters with this woman who, in half an hour's time, would dress and step out alone into the night through the back door, making her way home as if this were the most natural thing in the world. He stared at her through the dark, his face very close to hers. She was ugly, no question, but he owed his sons to her.

TWENTY-FIVE

His sons. In 1907 there were two of them; both in good health, but still too small for one to get any distinct sense of their characters. For the moment, despite what people say about blood being thicker than water, they were still strangers to Alphonse. This was a thought that he kept to himself. His friend the vet, for one, made it clear that he felt differently. He already made efforts to communicate with these strangers; he talked to them in their language, imitating its guttural sounds with ease. Bending together over the baby's crib or the elder boy's cot, he and Agnès were the very picture of marital stability, while, from the outside, leaning against the dresser smoking his cigar (the reason he was forbidden to come closer), Alphonse looked on with a kind of tender affection.

He pondered the strangeness of those two conceptions, and a quality they possessed which he could only describe as crossfire. In his case maternity and paternity had, for some reason, travelled along subterranean channels, only to emerge in precisely the spot where everybody expected to find them, in accordance with a law as old as the earth itself. But somewhere in those channels there was a deviation noticeable only to Alphonse – and not because his eye was any sharper.

When the villagers complimented Agnès on her children, the father's contribution was always remarked upon:

"They're the image of him!" everybody said.

The consoling nature of this comment was transparent. At this age, babies can look like anybody: they are still so bland

and so neutral; what was clear was that people felt the need to confirm – to Alphonse in particular – that his contribution to the act of creation was branded on the features of the little ones.

It had been a minimal, circumscribed and precisely aimed contribution. That was the truth, which it was only fair to recognise: when he had willed it, his sons had become flesh. In this respect, Agnès was the most receptive woman one could wish for; Courrier had been aware of this since the earliest days of their marriage.

These compliments about the children . . . On reflection, there was something unnerving about them, laced as they were with a certain menacing suspense. When people admired the older son's beauty (which, to be frank, Alphonse could not see at all), they would add a wish that he might also be healthy . . . But of course he would be! And good, as well . . . It was as if they were saying:

"Don't think you've got away with it completely, my friend – the difficult part is yet to come."

Good wishes are so laden with insinuation.

In any case he knew it better than anyone: the fact that his son might turn out to be handsome was entirely a matter of mathematics and chemistry. Men can claim no credit in this field, and Alphonse would have been the last to try to do so. The question of whether the child would grow up to be healthy and good was a more complex one, and it was in this area that his fellow villagers were hoping to catch him out.

How would his sons turn out? He began to wonder about it himself: would they be fastidious, like their mother, or broad-minded like their father? The mixture of their two characters had to be considered in all its nuances, taking into account indirect influences: surrogate mother and father figures which the two boys would meet along the way. Germaine had been a nonentity, a foreign body which was immediately expelled. The vet, on the other hand, was the grain of sand which insinuates itself into the valves of the oyster. Most importantly he was gentle; he looked after the potential pearls and did not seem to irritate the epidermis of the mother. Agnès had begun to call him "the Doctor", with easy deference. Far be it from Alphonse to feel jealousy. On the contrary, in his darker moods he would be visited by the veiled feeling that he had used Agnès as some sort of glorified container.

But he would recover from this immediately, because in the end everything is for the best, particularly in Alphonse Courrier's philosophy. After all, he had given his wife two sons and a recognised position in village society – a prestigious position. Everything is relative; once, a long time ago, his mother had been given a red dress she never knew what to do with.

TWENTY-SIX

In 1908 Courrier was forty-one. 1908, incidentally, was the year my father was born, and I feel I owe him a belated welcome. This doesn't contribute to my story in any way, but I have the feeling he'd have liked to receive it.

Enough of that. Let's get back to business. In 1908, to all appearances, nothing happened to Alphonse Courrier. His children were three and two respectively. They were well-brought-up boys, who were beginning to spend some time around their father. A father who thought he noticed, in direct proportion to their growth, a growing tenderness for the woman who had brought them about: Adèle Joffre.

At this point, one might be justified in wondering how, in a village comprising such a limited number of souls (some of them overbearingly curious souls), the secret liaison between Alphonse Courrier and Adèle Joffre could possibly have remained a secret. It wasn't just a matter of being careful – in some cases caution merely sharpens the wits of a gossip. No, it was a question of method.

Let's summarise the situation so far. Every Tuesday and Friday, barring illness – which was rare – the couple met in the dark and consummated their relationship. At times it was no more than an exchange of tender caresses and whispered words. Courrier was beginning to talk to Adèle so, in this sense, things had changed slightly. In her Alphonse had found a tenacious, thoughtful listener, and the seeds of a mental intimacy had insinuated themselves between their bodies, which until then had contained the sum total of their mutual understanding. This was a danger which Alphonse had never guarded against – he had never thought it necessary. As for Adèle, she feared nothing for herself, except in the matter of keeping a secret which she considered vital to Alphonse.

And yet, if you set your mind to it, a secret can more easily be kept in a village than in a big city. In a village everything is circumscribed, and rumours have such short journeys to make from house to house that they run no risk of getting lost along the way. It is the urge to communicate which acts as an amplifier for everything, even for things which you believed you wanted to keep under lock and key. You thought you wanted a secret but, when it came to it, you did not – that is all. Germaine was a case in point: in the days of the red dress it was common knowledge that the girl was in love with Alphonse Courrier, because she herself had sent signals to that effect throughout the village. Now it was equally well known that she had resigned herself to marrying a carter in a nearby village. It could not remain a secret (her resignation, rather than her marriage) because the feeling of suffocation that would have gripped her if she hadn't hinted at it to at least one person, would have killed her. And that one person made sure they found another, and so on and so forth. There is nothing original about this observation: it is already a commonplace in literature, as well as in real life.

Alphonse had nothing to communicate to anybody. At present he was perfectly in balance with his giving and receiving of happiness, so silence on the subject came quite naturally and was not at all hard to maintain.

Inevitably somebody had commented, in a concerned tone, to Agnès:

"Your husband really works too hard. Sometimes that shop light stays on till late at night."

"Oh, it's not just work," Madame Courrier had replied with a smile. "At times I think that shop is his living-room."

When they heard she was saying this herself, all malicious gossip died on their lips.

Germaine too had entered that living-room, but in broad daylight, and a long time after she had stopped working for the Courriers. The curtains in her mother's house needed hooks. While she waited for the shopkeeper to assemble her order, the girl looked nostalgically around the shop, then, at Courrier's smiling request: "That will be two francs and thirty centimes, please, Germaine," she burst into uncontrollable sobs, pausing only to make sure nobody was hanging around in the vicinity of the front door.

Alphonse looked at her in amazement. Women's tears always surprise men, or at least embarrass them. This time Alphonse had the added problem of whether to reach out a comforting hand – which would, it was now clear, compound the damage – or to look on sympathetically as her grief burnt itself out. He found no more satisfactory response than to lean his elbows on the counter and take his head in his hands, re-emerging with a mournful cry of:

"Good Lord, child! What on earth can have happened?"

Germaine's bosom was heaving with sobs, and it was a far from negligible bosom. Courrier reached out and tapped her hand gently, whispering close to her ear:

"Well?"

"I'm getting married," she stammered, mangling these simple words almost beyond recognition.

"I know you are, Germaine. Marriage is what all you girls want. If anything, I'd have thought you've left it a bit late. What's the problem? Do you need money?"

The girl's squint was at its most frenzied as she turned her eyes to the man she had loved, and whom she had believed capable, in his own way, of loving her in return. Because Alphonse, as far as Germaine was concerned, really had been in love with her, and it was only his sense of duty towards his family – those two sons she hated from the bottom of her heart, the eldest most of all, even though he was her godson – which had prevented him from abandoning himself to adventure in her arms. It does not take much to turn love into hate. It is enough to notice, on just one occasion, an unconvincing tone of voice or an unfortunate remark. In this case, the remark was:

"Do you need money?"

Poison flooded the veins of the carter's betrothed.

Let us pause for a moment here, because Germaine had imagined this encounter differently. In her plans, she had been going to enter the shop, ask for the hooks, then burst into tears – and, up until this point, everything had gone perfectly. Then Courrier – carried away by her emotion and by the sorrow he had been repressing ever since her engagement had become public – was supposed, for the first and only time, to embrace and kiss her. That would have been enough, and Germaine's life, her sacrificial marriage, everything, would have had a meaning. It would have become one of those memories which remain permanently ingrained in one's past, a source of solace in times of trouble. It happens often enough in literature, so why not in life?

Through her tears, she searched for the two francs thirty centimes. Then, her sobs abating like a thunderstorm which is beginning to pass over, she stammered:

"I've got the money," referring to the small bill she was paying now, but also to her impending marriage and the house she was going to, in that other village where, thank God, there were no ironmongers.

"Germaine." Alphonse's lips pressed around a whisper of

tenderness verging on the maudlin. The image of her once-bitter rival flashed before her eyes, and she heard again the sound of the slap which had horrified her, like a desecration. She too stretched out her hand, but only to snatch up the packet of hooks. She turned away abruptly, slipped awkwardly off her clog, and felt her ankle twist painfully.

She finished her crying in the street.

TWENTY-SEVEN

"Another glass?"

"No, thank you."

"Sensible man!" sighed Alphonse. "Not that you'll live much longer than the rest of us – my wife is sensible too, and clever. She knows a lot about a lot of things, both in general and in particular."

"Particular in what sense?"

"About me, dear doctor. She knows everything about me."

"I'd have thought that was normal in a married couple. Obviously I'm no expert in these things, but . . ."

"But she knows everything. Quite so."

Courrier's blue eyes were ever so slightly clouded, and his voice sounded unusually fragile, about to crack at any moment. The level of Calvados in the bottle in front of him had sunk worryingly. This was the first time the vet had seen his friend in anything less than total control. It was strange – as if, let's say, Alphonse were standing in front of him wearing a jacket and tie but no trousers. It wasn't like him.

Alphonse reached for the bottle again, grasped it with slightly trembling hand, then put it back down abruptly without pouring from it. He straightened his back, removed his glasses and passed a hand over his eyes. He appeared to pull himself together.

"I'm sounding a bit the worse for wear, aren't I?" he asked.

The vet nodded, embarrassed.

"Ask me why. I never do this. I never drink, I mean. I've

never had too much to drink in all my life, but the way I feel at the moment, I'm tempted to carry on a bit longer to find out what happens when you lose your head completely. Through alcohol, I mean." He paused theatrically. "You know, don't you, that Germaine is getting married? You know she's going away? And did you know the girl came to my shop in tears? No, of course you didn't. Tears in a hardware shop! Slightly less poetic than weeping in a stable. I'm sorry, it must be your being here that made me think of stables. I'm sorry. I'm quite sober now. Do you know why Germaine is getting married?"

The vet still hadn't recovered from the stable analogy; he may not even have fully understood the reference to himself – but no, he didn't know why Germaine was getting married.

"Because all women marry, doctor, and so should all men. I did my duty, when the time came. Now it's you" – here Alphonse wagged a finger at his companion – "who's letting the side down. I did my duty: I had two sons. All you do is cling to other people's sons. I'm not reproaching you, my friend. You are quite welcome to everything I own, the whole lot. Please take it." Courrier bowed slightly, in a clownish homage to the vet.

"Alphonse, you sound as if you've gone completely mad. And what has Germaine got to do with anything?"

"Ah, precisely. We were talking about why Germaine is going to marry a man she doesn't like. It's true that the girl hasn't got much choice, but this choice wasn't hers." He lowered his voice like a true conspirator, and beckoned the reluctant vet closer. "It was made by our little Agnès Courrier, née Duval," he whispered. "My wife."

I must have forgotten to mention where this surprising tableau of a drunken Alphonse and a sober vet was taking place; against what background we should picture them, and in what colours. But the answer is not hard to guess: the shop, at night, in the dim light of the oil lamp, which threw golden shadows and amber tones onto the faces of the two men, leaving the rest of the scene shrouded in darkness. A perfect Flemish painting; I might even venture "Jeremiah's vision", but in any case a Rembrandt, however minor. But then again, it cannot be all that minor, if it has to portray the consternation which was now spreading across the face of the vet.

"Alphonse! It's as if you were accusing your wife of scheming to . . ." he said.

"It's not 'as if', nor is it an accusation. The more time goes by, the more impressed I am by that woman's skill in weaving her plots, like the perfect house spider, which never once misses its target with its spittle. I'm lost in admiration, my dear friend." This time Alphonse toasted his words with a drink, then continued:

"Since you're more in contact with my wife than I am, would you please convey my sincerest respects to her? I'll do the same in person, later on."

"What are you saying?" asked the vet. "That you're not speaking to each other?"

"Of course we're speaking. In our house, harmony reigns; our sons are growing up in perfect serenity. That is precisely why I don't pay her that kind of compliment directly. Serenity requires silence, tact and reserve. Each to his own, in his own house. The fact that the house happens to be the same one, doesn't mean either partner should use it in a way that is too indiscreet or too personal."

The Flemish painting was beginning to look like "Las Meniñas": an illusory foreground which directs the eye to a mirror, in which one can see the protagonists of the real painting, who nevertheless escape the viewer's notice – and so on and so forth. The vet was largely unacquainted with the world of fine art, and this portrait of the Courrier family was becoming horribly confusing. Suddenly, he thought he'd been struck by a revelation: Agnès Courrier had been jealous of the ugly Germaine, to the extent of deliberately removing her from the village. Jealousy can spring from the most unexpected sources.

"But she isn't exactly jealous of me, doctor," said Alphonse. The vet started. Alphonse seemed to have read his thoughts.

"That isn't the heart of the matter," Alphonse continued. "She's just annoyed by the buzz of insignificant flies. Flies are harmless, but they're a nuisance – particularly when we kill one, and ten more come along to take its place. Still, we go on killing the one which comes into range, deluding ourselves that its death is an example to others. She labours skilfully, my house spider. Once she decides to strike, Agnès' aim is infallible, and her choice of weapon is even more deadly: a wedding! That's enough," he said, pushing the bottle away. "No more of that tonight."

Silence fell over the tableau: a long, obstinate silence. But Alphonse hadn't exhausted his material: he still had a dab of pigment on his brush. He worked it well; he diluted it in preparation for the final flourish; he wet it with the humours of his lachrymose, drunken mood. Then he placed his last brushmark on the canvas:

"You see, doctor, it's only ever flies that get swatted."

TWENTY-EIGHT

The scene is the village, just before the wedding. A village is a social structure founded, for better or worse, on sharing: villages participate in one's life, even more than one participates in them.

She got married in the spring, of course: in April 1909. She refused to have Alphonse Courrier as a witness. She even tried not to invite him, but that was asking too much of her mother's patience and would have been too lavish of a gift to the village gossips. The Courriers, complete with children, would be there – if not in the front row, at least in a good seat – and they would play their part well.

Agnès made it her business to choose the wedding present: a china teapot from a city shop, which looked as if it hadn't come cheap. Alphonse made it his to keep a low profile, which he was sure would be easy: his wife provided excellent cover. He took advantage of his supporting role to concentrate on the ceremony – something he hadn't done even during his own wedding. He listened attentively to the old priest's words; he heard the solemn tone which descended on all the participants and which, by some mysterious alchemy, cut him to the quick. Adèle Joffre was somewhere in that church. The bride and groom exchanged rings; there were no children with cushions this time. The carter pulled the wedding-rings unceremoniously out of his pocket.

It was at this point that Alphonse began to twist his own wedding-ring; slowly, laboriously, until, dislodged from its customary position, it made a bid for freedom. In the deep silence, there was a sudden tinkling and a flash of gold, as the ring hit the stone flags of the dark church. It then began to roll, shooting out from under the Courriers' pew and careering cheerfully into middle of the nave.

After that early unpleasantness with the runny nose, this was the second accursed episode in the life of Alphonse Courrier.

The entire congregation, including Alphonse, turned its attention to the gold wedding-ring lying on the floor. In the ensuing buzz of voices, everyone made their reaction plain, whether overtly or not – their response could, in any case, be gleaned from the sniggers and curious stares. I doubt whether anyone present had heard of the theories of Sigmund Freud. The doctor in question had not yet attained his present fame, and naturally a village in the Auvergne is not the easiest place for such a reputation to penetrate. But even without the help of Sigmund Freud and his theories about unconscious slips, everybody managed to draw the obvious conclusion about this well-respected shopkeeper who, in the middle of a wedding, at the very moment when the rings are being exchanged, had thrown his own to the ground in such a sensational fashion.

Alphonse, it is only fair to admit, had not thrown the ring: it had slipped off his finger. But even the simplest, most uneducated of villagers knew that every effect has a cause, and that every material cause is produced by an impulse, a deep-seated drive. If Alphonse Courrier had lost his ring while Germaine accepted hers, binding herself forever to the carter, the two events could not be unrelated, whether the clever Alphonse had intended it or not.

Agnès – cleverer than he – gently pushed little Georges forwards and, indicating the object of everybody's attention, urged him to pick it up and return it to his father. The child toddled down the aisle and came back with the ring.

Everything returned to normal, and the priest went on with the service, but the atmosphere was no longer the same. Madame Chinot had to content herself with elbowing her husband in the ribs, casting a meaningful glance at her neighbour, and smiling suggestively at her daughter in the pew behind. She was forced to stop there, for the time being, having no other method of communication at her disposal. Speech was out of the question under the circumstances, but she would make up for that later. For the moment all she needed to do was tack in a rough outline: the embroidery could wait.

I won't go into the unspoken thoughts of Madame Alphonse Courrier, who – as the child handed the ring back to his father – leant down to stroke Georges' hair in a gesture of infinite tenderness and gratitude, while, with her other hand, she gripped Alain's small arm so convulsively that he felt as if it were being crushed in a vice. She did not look at her husband even for an instant, but noticed, out of the corner of her eye, that he had not put his ring back on. In his confusion he had thrust it into his pocket.

The church was a small one, yet, overflowing as it was with people, it would take a long time to consider every guest's reading of the incident, from the most obvious to the most convoluted. Not even the red dress at the christening, a few years earlier, had caused such a stir.

During the reception, which took place under the pergola at the local inn, where there were drinks set out on tables in the warm sun, nobody raised the subject – either seriously or in jest – with the most significantly interested party, although it was the only topic of conversation among his guests. The village had never seen such an entertaining, successful wedding.

Germaine took her leave, on her husband's cart, at the end of a memorable day. She left behind her a community in a whirl of excitement and carried with her, to her new village and her new home, an improbable illusion. She had no longer dared to hope, especially after her humiliation in the shop, she really hadn't – and yet, at the critical point in her wedding ceremony, Monsieur Courrier had thrown away his ring. Seated on her husband's rickety cart – magnificently decorated for the occasion – she rode out of the village in triumph. She was taking with her what she believed she had the right to consider a veiled declaration of love.

There is nothing like feeling loved to make one well disposed towards others, even that obtrusive other who was her husband, Jacques Lavalle. Consequently, she followed him with the blithe equanimity of someone who has got what she wanted. And who got it in front of the whole village, in spite of stern Madame Courrier, over whom she felt she had won an exemplary victory. That evening, in her new home, she let her husband do as he wished, as if the whole business had nothing to do with her. Body and soul are so easily divorced.

As for the carter, Jacques Lavalle, he never doubted for a moment that the day had gone perfectly. He can't have seen or heard anything of Alphonse Courrier's ring.

TWENTY-NINE

From April 1909 to the beginning of 1910, Alphonse Courrier's business flourished. It appeared to be prospering for a variety of reasons, all of which were linked by invisible connections. Since Germaine had left her birthplace comforted – one might even say fulfilled – by her fate, her adoptive village began to show a new regard for the ironmonger's shop, which the recent bride described to her neighbours with impassioned authority.

"I used to work there," she would say loftily. "I know it well. Whatever you ask for, he'll have it. He must be very clever to keep such a big place going." And she basked in the reflected glory. She would have liked a few more questions, but for whatever reason (envy, a surfeit of information, or curiosity otherwise appeased) her new friends never seemed to want to know any more from her. She would be left standing there, with a far-away look on her face, remembering the scene of her passion – a scene she would happily have described in detail. As it was, the other women procured that detail for themselves, by sending husbands and brothers to the shop and then tormenting them with questions which the men were hardly able to answer, unaware as they were of their role as spies. The husbands and brothers, however, continued to patronise the shop, thus widening the circle of Courrier's clientèle.

Germaine's new village was set high in the hills, and overlooked a landscape very different from the one she was accustomed to. Her native village lay in a dip, surrounded by spent craters filled with deep lakes. Its houses stood so close together that you could spy on your neighbour merely by looking through your window. Germaine's house, on the other hand – her new house – had one whole side overlooking the valley and the road which wound down through the fields towards her previous home. At the bottom, just before a bend hid the road from view, you could make out the Joffre workshop: a large, protruding building, on the border between the two villages. Germaine's more frequent toings and froings between the villages, particularly in the early days of her marriage, led her to skirt the walls of the large house which she had previously hardly even noticed. Occasionally she cast an absent-minded glance towards the courtyard and the carpentry shop. It was a large yard, full of planed boards piled high under a projecting roof, and sacks filled with wood-shavings and sawdust.

The place was always dusty, and so were the men who worked in it. Not dirty – dusty. Their sister, that Adèle whom Germaine knew only vaguely – as did everyone else in the village, for that matter – was covered in the same dust. Even though she no longer helped in the shop, as she had in her youth, she would never be free of the smell of freshly-sawn wood which pervaded the whole house – she smelt of it herself. She and Germaine barely exchanged nods. The new bride felt rather superior, and considered that she had very little in common with the ungainly spinster nobody had wanted.

I don't know if this is a sociologically proven condition, but women appear to be transformed by marriage. The pale, cross-eyed girl was gaining exponentially in self-esteem, and self-esteem engenders changes: in expression, tone of voice, even posture. The world had assigned her a place, had recog-nised her as being somebody's, (I don't know whether it is only women, or humans in general, who have this odd belief that, to be somebody, you have to belong to somebody), and conferred on her the role, if not the title, of Madame. Germaine became conceited. She dispensed an affected bonhomie to all and sundry; she flaunted her happiness. She had grasped the social aspect of marriage. As for its other aspect – emotion – she couldn't yet see the point of it. So satisfied was she with her new condition, that she even forgot to love Alphonse Courrier. But by the time that happened, she had already done a lot of good for his shop.

"I'm always so busy with the house: my husband's family spoilt him, and I have to keep things just the same. The cleaning, the cooking – everything has to be just the way his mother did it," she was saying one day, with an affected sigh, as she waited to be served by Madame Chinot. She still went there because she trusted the Chinots, and because she had more to say to her old village about married life, than she did to the new about being single.

"You're lucky, Germaine: you have a nice house, a good husband. Your mother is in good health, and you've got away from a gossiping village," Madame Chinot replied in a low voice.

"Gossiping?" the girl repeated curiously. For a moment she regressed to the insecurity which made her eyes wander.

"Heavens, dear child, nobody would ever have thought you were the type to stir up such a hornet's nest – and always in church too!"

Germaine regained control of her eyes. Of course: the christening, all those years ago, and her wedding, with its strange aftermath of speculation –

"They can't still be talking about all that, can they?" she asked.

Madame Chinot sighed. She wound a ribbon, which had

once been white, around her finger, then unwound it again; rolled it tightly up around itself, and placed it neatly into her apron pocket.

"You went away," she said. "You've been able to forget all about it, but us here, we've been left wondering. Have you ever had the chance, with the Courriers, to – ?"

Germaine had genuinely forgotten that she ever loved him. She felt herself flush, but only for an instant. No, she hadn't seen the Courriers again, except through the window of her mother's house. They had exchanged greetings, and once she was sure she had noticed a tender look from Alphonse. But all that belonged to the past.

"No," she replied. "And – how are they?"

Another deep sigh from Madame Chinot. The Courriers were a thorn in her side. They'd been leaving her on tenterhooks, groping for certainties, ever since the days of the poor old lady: that way she'd had of saying and not saying, of not having the courage to open up a little – between friends, for God's sake, between friends! And this new Madame Courrier (new in a manner of speaking, by now), she was even worse. Stubborn and proud. For the first time in her life, Germaine found herself thinking that Madame Courrier's pride might be a good thing. She had learnt a lot from her former mistress.

Soon afterwards, she left the butcher's wife preparing to close the shop, and walked across the village square. She cast a glance at the ironmonger's, with its half-closed door. It was late, on a warm, inviting autumn evening. The carter would still be at work, and Germaine knew the road home by heart, so she could take her time. There was no hurry.

She knocked on the shop door and pushed it open without waiting for a reply. It was dark inside the shop; the glow from Alphonse's cigar and the gold of his glasses shone through the gloom. Behind the lenses the dark blue of two

surprised eyes moved restlessly. Even his voice sounded dark:
"Oh, hello, Germaine. What brings you here at this hour?"

"I was just passing," she replied. "I was on my way home,
so I thought I'd stop in to say hello, Alphonse."

("She called me Alphonse," he said to his wife as they sat
together at the table. "Imagine – next time it'll be 'Alphonse
dearest'." And Agnès, her teacher, gave the tiniest nod of
approval – whether at her husband's surprise or at her pupil's
progress, it is impossible to say.)

In the old days, Courrier's silent response to Germaine's
words would have crushed her spirit. No longer. It was she
who took control of the situation, walking up to the counter
in a confident manner and lifting her arm, slowly and provoca-
tively, to rearrange the bun at the nape of her neck. Courrier
was cautious.

"You're looking well," he said. "You've even put on some
weight. So you're walking home on your own? Or is your
husband coming to pick you up? It's already dark." He glanced
at the bunch of keys dangling from his belt. "I was just about
to close."

"My husband comes home late on Tuesdays," Germaine said.
"He has a longer delivery run. He never gets back before eleven."

One might almost have thought that the overtures which the
insipid Germaine would never have dared to make, were, on
the contrary, well within the repertoire of Madame Lavalle.

"So that's what a wedding is for!" was Courrier's thought. But
it was his thought alone, and it was malevolent. Little Germaine
was simply savouring the exhilaration of not quaking in his
presence, of not trembling with emotion. Far more satisfying
than making advances!

She looked at him steadily – despite one of her eyes' apparent fascination with the shelves on the left of the room – and
smiled broadly, erasing the memory of the tears she had shed

on her previous visit. Then she stepped away from the counter, saying:

"Anyway, I'd best be off. It gets chilly at this time of night. Take care of yourself, Alphonse."

Let us imagine an aerial view of the building which contained Alphonse Courrier's shop. The door on to the square swings shut behind the robust figure of a woman, who walks away, swaying her hips. Round the back, along the narrow, ill-lit alleyway that runs parallel to that side of the square, another woman, dressed in black, approaches the shop and slips through the half-open door. The first woman, meanwhile, suddenly veers right and glances down the alleyway behind the shop: unfortunately for her, just a moment too late.

THIRTY

And now let us pause for a moment, to take, if we can, an overall view of the situation so far, and to assess the positions of each piece on the chess-board. In literature, chess is often used as an image at moments like this, but it is an old-fashioned and tedious image, and one that has become too transparently metaphorical. Why not another game – billiards, for example? Let us imagine that Alphonse Courrier's village is a billiard-table (not quite as smooth, of course, but then it wouldn't be as perfectly squared off as a chess-board either). The large ivory balls, scattered around the table, indicate that a game has already begun; our task is to try to understand what the players are doing.

Of course the anthropomorphism of chess-men is more convincing – and nobler in appearance – than the round shape of a ball against the green baize. For various reasons, however, I am quite certain that chess requires no more intelligence than the ballistic calculations of the expert billiard-player. Calculations which have to combine manual dexterity, a steady hand and a good eye. Alone, lit by the beam from the over-head lamp framing the large table, the player employs both mind and body; he requires both an accurate aim and complex powers of reasoning. A man playing the game with skill is a pleasure to watch: he moves around the table with aquatic slowness, then all of a sudden he concentrates, gathers his strength, and darts the cue towards the projectile. Everything happens in an instant. In a fraction of a second, he shatters the stillness of the landscape on the table, and unleashes a turbulent motion: if he is a good player, he unleashes it precisely as he intended.

Few other activities harness this static energy, then convert it so effectively into action. Let us consider the scene a moment later, when the last echoes of the seismic shock are lost in the stillness once each ball stops rolling. Like a city which has just been through an earthquake, the green table lies in a state of suspense, waiting for the next tremor to disrupt its order once more.

What I am trying to say by all this is that, rather than a chess-board, Alphonse Courrier's village might better be likened to one of those splendid pieces of furniture which take pride of place in the country houses of the English aristocracy – standing peacefully for as long as the cues remain in their rack.

The aerial view which I happened to mention earlier, could now shed light on a possibility undiscernible from the level of the baize. If the Player (the hypothetical arbiter of fate who governs the lives of men), had played his shot a fraction of a second earlier, the ball representing Germaine would have collided with Adèle's ball, or would have seen it roll inexorably towards the pocket of Alphonse's shop door. What then? It does not need much imagination to realize how fierce a tremor would have shaken the length and breadth of the table.

The pleasure of clandestine relationships is often enhanced by the fact that one is denying knowledge to others. For some people this is an exercise in power, as gratifying as boasting. Locked safely away in their secret, they avoid the judgment of others, while continuing to pass judgment themselves. Courrier had always found this position of secrecy a congenial one, but he had used it magnanimously. In fact, the second half of the exercise wasn't his sort of thing at all: he did not judge others. At most he might understand them, being well equipped to do so. The motive for his secrecy was not a desire for power. Neither did it spring from a fear of being judged – not entirely, in any case. It was just natural reserve: a quality which is in danger of extinction. Why should he flaunt his intimacy with a woman? Social convention had imposed its levy, and collected it. His contribution to the continuation of the species had been effected. Nobody could have asked him for more. To say that Courrier felt at ease with the world would be an understatement: he felt at ease with his own conscience, which is far more important.

But later on that evening, Alphonse was not able to do justice to his relationship with Adèle. He admitted defeat honestly, then lay there, surprised and sullen, accepting her consoling caresses. For perhaps the first time in his life, fear – or the possibility of fear – had flashed through his mind and paralysed him. His blood had run cold at the thought that someone – not necessarily his wife, but someone – might discover the secret he had harboured for years.

He could feel Adèle's rough palms passing gently over his hair and neck, again and again. She was caressing him in the precise, methodical way in which people stroke an animal, because there is no other way to communicate.

"It's not a good idea for me to come here on Friday evenings," she said.

"Eh?" he inquired, almost unable to articulate even a grunt.

"I'm not running any risks. And even if I . . . I wouldn't care. But you: you've got a wife, two children – the whole village knows you." She stroked him again, running her hand the wrong way over the hair at the nape of his neck.

"The whole village knows you too," he replied. "What about your brothers?"

He propped himself up on an elbow, pulling away from her a little to see her as Adèle Joffre, the woman who lived on the outskirts of the village with her two brothers: the old maid nobody had wanted.

At such close quarters, without his glasses, she looked blurred and misty. We all know (though I don't know whether Courrier knew it) that the gods of ancient Greece did not willingly reveal themselves to mortals; the God of Moses, too, stayed up in the mist and clouds on Mount Sinai. Things that men held sacred were shut away in a chamber at the heart of the temple, hidden from view.

What was the most sacred thing in Alphonse Courrier's life? He hesitated for a moment before saying it, even to himself: some words do not come easily. The thing he held most sacred was Adèle Joffre.

"Very well, then. Not Fridays," he said.

He watched her get dressed, unhurriedly: saw her abandon her woman's figure to the folds of an ugly black skirt. He accompanied her to the door, looking carefully up and down the deserted alleyway. What a miracle that, in all those years, not one of the windows overlooking the street had ever had a light in it.

THIRTY-ONE

Alphonse Courrier's sons might seem to have been forgotten in a corner. And yet they are still there, and they are growing, in the care of a mother who is strict but fair, supported by a dependable father.

By now they must have been around four and five respectively, and they were at that insolent phase: the age when you have to love children very much not to find them annoying. This is a general observation, but, more specifically, it is also true that each historical period – as well as each social class – has its own type of child, with its own particular brand of insolence. An early twentieth-century photograph and an eighteenth-century portrait, when compared, will – just through the facial expressions – speak volumes about the way everything changes over time, even childhood.

The Courrier sons, born at the turn of the century, were, in every sense, children poised between two worlds. They were leaving one century behind, while the new one was still unsteady on its feet – so much so, that it even stumbled into a war. What is more – to return to the young Courriers – their position in society was an ambivalent one. Neither rich nor poor, they were in danger of being lonely, falling as they did between two stools. But they had a wise guide in their mother. Madame Courrier saw their lives as a long-term investment. An investment that involved making choices about how, and with whom, they should grow up.

The village did have some truly rich families, and it was on them that Madame Courrier focused. But nobody could have found fault with her sense of measure. Contact with these families had to be limited, and established by invitation only – she had carefully explained this principle to her sons, despite their young age, and had discovered a way to drive it into them. If, having once sampled the wealth of toys available to their more prosperous neighbours, the little ones gravitated towards them, their mother would strike terror into their hearts by raising her eyebrows in a manner which conveyed such alarm, such fury, such unfathomable menace, that it immediately stifled all protest. They would turn back, conscious of having narrowly escaped some peril, and end up playing on their own. They couldn't run around in the street like most of the village children, because they were too well dressed. Neither could they become embroiled in scraps in the dust, or expeditions into the woods around the village: it would have been unthinkable to be caught with muddy shoes by their prosperous neighbours. So, most of the time, they were drawn into the orbit of the rich, awaiting a summons. This longed-for sign might come at any moment, from the window of the large house in the square, or from a servant who glimpsed them through the front door. You had to be ready. Statistically, over the course of, let's say, a week, such invitations were extremely rare, yet the two little Courriers could not bring themselves to escape that tragic oscillation between waiting and boredom – a state with which they were in danger of becoming far too familiar.

Until, one day, the vet took them with him on his rounds. Strictly speaking the boys' father should have been the one to take their dilemma in hand – especially since his shop, being in the square, was an ideal place to get noticed. But children weren't really Alphonse's thing. Probably he didn't understand them.

In any case, the vet turned up one morning, on the cart he used for his longer rounds. He knocked on the door with his riding whip, and stepped straight into the kitchen, catching Agnès unprepared – which simply means that her hair was hanging loose and uncombed, and she was wearing the previous day's less-than-perfect apron. It is a fallacy that women are more seductive first thing in the morning. What is seductive is the almost inevitable mental connection with the image of bed. A connection which the vet made precisely on cue.

Which is not to say that any other woman would have had the same effect on him as Agnès did, at that moment – most definitely not. Certainly, however, Agnès had looked prettier on hundreds of occasions. She herself was painfully aware of her state of disarray, and felt ill at ease, to the point of addressing her visitor somewhat abruptly. Then she fell silent, discerning, in the narrowing of his eyes, an intent his features had never before expressed. This was entirely beyond Madame Courrier's experience: years of marriage had not yet taught her about this side of the male character. The two looked at each other for a fraction of a second: time enough for the most fortunate woman in the village to realize that there existed in the world a dark abyss of happiness which she had not yet chanced to penetrate.

"The boys will be ready in a moment," Agnès said, breathlessly.

"So you don't mind if I take them out for a few hours?" the vet asked, in a similarly agitated voice.

"No, no, of course not. I'm sure they'll have much more fun with you than cooped up here in the house with me. I'll go and see if they're getting dressed." She paused for a moment before leaving the room – just long enough to give him time to seize her arm in a grip which melted her.

"Heavenly Father!" murmured Agnès, as she pulled her mouth away from the doctor's.

"Dear God!" he exclaimed.

They both turned to the half-open door; fortunately there was no-one there.

The children had an outing they would never forget. They travelled the length and breadth of the countryside in the vet's cart, visited two or three farms, and forgot all about their neat clothes and the fact that their shoes were unsuitable for dusty fields and manure-filled stables. They were delivered back home at midday, and Alphonse was there to meet them.

THIRTY-TWO

He swung the boys down from the cart, keeping them well away from his nose. Half-disgusted, half-amused, he exclaimed:

"They stink like goats! If you don't hurry up and get clean, you're not eating with me today, is that clear?" Then, turning to the vet, who was still sitting up on the cart, he added:

"I don't know what kind of a state you're in, but if you can get by with just washing your hands, you're welcome to stay to lunch. I'll tell Agnès to set an extra place. If you don't mind a simple lunch . . ." He gave a sidelong look at the vet. Alphonse's golden face was lit by the sun, which shone in his eyes, forcing him to squint.

Alphonse Courrier was standing at his front door, inviting an old friend to an informal lunch, just as he had hundreds of times before. But to the other man everything looked and sounded unfamiliar. Beyond the doorway in which Courrier stood, lay the unknown: the woman who, for years now, had graciously cooked her exquisite dishes for him as well as for her family; the woman whose children he had loved as tenderly as if they were his own; the woman whose cool beauty had conquered him, and reduced him to years of admiring silence. After this morning, that woman could not fail to betray the signs of a cosmic shift, which he, the elderly vet, could not bear to witness; not in the presence of her husband.

"Well then? Agnès is waiting for an answer."

The vet was struck by the suspicion that Alphonse might be issuing a challenge: he brought his wife's name into play as though it were nothing special. The vet's rival – for such was Alphonse's new role – was luring him into a treacherous game, fully aware that the older man was at his mercy. Well, if he was a man, if he – at almost sixty years old – was a real man, he had to accept that challenge.

He climbed off the cart with the heavy legs of an old man and the nerves of an adolescent. He went in.

By contrast with the light outside, it always seems darker indoors; in the shadows which enveloped the vet as he entered, the poor man recognised a symbol for his confused state of mind.

So there they were, sitting at the table, all three unaware of the fact that, for the first time, they were on an equal footing: they all had something to hide, something to fear, something to make them happy. Three improbable Arthurian knights – if one can stretch this comparison to include the woman. A woman who – despite having been left in quite a different state that morning – now shone in her full splendour. Her hair was held up with pins, and she was wearing a snow-white apron. Unusually, before sitting down, she untied the apron, and let it fall limply over the back of a chair, revealing a cream blouse, which was buttoned up to the neck and tucked into a skirt. This last garment was dark and of uncertain hue, but matched her top perfectly. Alphonse looked at her curiously, but made no comment. It was not like him to pry, though it was very like him to notice. The vet thanked heaven for her neutral tidiness after the disarray she'd been in that morning. It gave him a chance to get his breath back, while Agnès – defying herself and her accustomed way of life – was fighting an inner battle between euphoria and dismay.

She hadn't welcomed her husband's rash invitation to the vet. She remembered the "Heavenly Father!" with which she had concluded the first real kiss of her life, and she asked herself, in her inexperience, whether she ought already to add the words "from my lover". She stifled the thought, then regretted stifling it. Sometimes the awareness that we have transgressed, however much it may trouble our conscience, generates priceless elation. After all, things should be called by their names; if they aren't, they can disappear. What was eluding her was the boundary beyond which the title of "lover" became truly relevant. And then? Once she had entered that territory, what unknown landscape awaited her?

In any case, when she heard that the vet was going to stay to lunch, she rushed upstairs to get changed. While the children splashed and yelled at the kitchen sink, she weighed up in an instant which would be the best outfit she could put on without veering too far from the ordinary. But what was ordinary, now that the course of her life had been jolted and changed? To cut a long story short, she chose her smartest clothes without even realizing it.

The men, as I mentioned earlier, very tactfully made no comment. The children, who were the only other danger, had – at last – more important things to think and talk about. Their tongues seemed to be the only part of their bodies not suffering from exhaustion.

At the end of an uninspiring lunch, as Agnès cleared the table, taking extra care not to stain her clothes, Alphonse produced a new cigar and offered it to the vet, who accepted.

"Are you sure?" Courrier asked in amazement. "Haven't you stopped smoking?"

"Yes, but since you're offering . . ."

"I always offer, and you always say no," Alphonse pointed out, eying the cigar wistfully. It was his second-to-last. He usually stocked up in town, going all the way to Clermont-Ferrand.

"I must say, you smoke good tobacco, Alphonse," the vet

commented a moment later, inhaling with relish. "I know it's not good for me," he added, almost to himself, "but it's only this once. The thing is to do everything in moderation, to know when to stop, and not let it become a habit, because then it stops being a pleasure," he concluded thoughtfully, "and becomes a disease . . ."

Courrier was watching him, smoking vigorously.

"One cigar leads to another," he said. "You wait and see. Cigars are like cherries."

The vet started slightly at this remark, as he'd just been drawing quite different conclusions about the power and tenacity of bad habits. Alphonse too suppressed a sigh: it was two o'clock on a Friday afternoon. Seven hours or so until nightfall. But there was no point in counting them.

That night, the village boasted three insomniacs. It is true that the vet lived elsewhere, but how can we exclude him from this temporary fraternity? His mind was there, wedged between the married couple, who shared the same darkness, each at pains not to suggest they were awake. In this particular subterfuge, Alphonse Courrier had a distinct advantage over his wife, who had not suffered from such an indisposition before, and consequently betrayed herself constantly. Her breathing was not heavy enough, for instance, and she moved much less than usual. In the belief that tossing and turning was a sure sign of insomnia, she lay stiff as a plank, as she never would have usually.

As for Alphonse – lying on his side, arms enclosing his chest in a sort of shell – he was chalking up his loneliness on his night-time blackboard. The sleepless woman at his side annoyed him: two symptoms of disorder at once – Adèle not there, and Agnès not asleep – were two symptoms too many. The second bothered him the most. Thoughts do not escape from our heads, that is certain, but the walls of the brain seem more permeable when another person is so very close.

The dawn light that filtered through the shutters revealed two pale faces with stubbornly closed eyes, and two rather stiff bodies, lying on a bed which looked hardly slept in.

THIRTY-THREE

Adèle Joffre, on the other hand, fell instantly into a deep and restful sleep. By the time her brothers had finished dinner, and she had cleared the table and washed up, it was still only eight-thirty; she had the whole evening to herself. Of course the same thing happened five times a week, but this extra evening felt like a gift. There is something inherently positive about breaking a habit, whatever the cause. Life takes a liberty; it takes a detour. However minimal, however trifling it may be, this change carries weight. Practically speaking, all it means is that, at a given hour, you find yourself dislocated, in a slightly unusual situation, so that you feel as if you have outwitted time and lured it out of position. It is a mild form of revenge, and one usually without consequence.

This was Adèle Joffre's experience on that Friday evening, when she discovered she was happy without Alphonse – or rather, she discovered the pleasure of thinking of him, at a time when she wouldn't normally be able to, because he would be beside her, in flesh and blood. She let herself drift into one of her deepest sleeps. It was early. It may not even have been properly dark. Yet she was already resting peacefully. And dreaming.

In her dream, she was the wife of Alphonse Courrier, the ironmonger, and the mother of two children whose faces she could not see, but whose bodies she felt between her fingers, as she squeezed their fragile arms. Since she was essentially a woman of limited horizons, the universe of her dream was restricted to a kitchen – a kitchen that was not her own, but was no better or worse. It must have been the Courriers'. She dreamt of doing something she had never been allowed to do for Alphonse. She dreamt of cooking for him, in the light of an unimaginably bright sun. She smelt the meat simmering peacefully on the hearth.

With each passing moment the sun burned more brightly, and its heat flooded the day – or was it night? – until the dream was engulfed in light: a blinding light, which burst in through the kitchen window and lit the room more brilliantly than a summer sun. It sounded strange, in that kitchen, to hear one of her brothers calling her with annoying persistence; he wouldn't leave her alone to get on with her chores; he kept raising his voice obsessively.

Finally she opened her burning eyes. Her throat was parched; her breath seemed to be getting stuck somewhere. It refused to come out. The voice was right on top of her now, and so were her brother Joseph's hands, as he lifted her bodily out of her dream, and out of her bedroom, which was engulfed in whitish smoke.

"For Christ's sake, Adèle, wake up. The whole house is on fire."

What? she tried to think to herself. What about the simmering stew, the sun, the fireplace, the light – then, since everything was muddled, and not even her lungs would obey her any more, Adèle gave up trying to understand. She slumped backwards, and her mouth gaped pointlessly.

Everything was shut down, everything was obstructed. Everything was over.

THIRTY-FOUR

A village roused abruptly is polyphonic. The ringing of the bell summoning the volunteer firemen – a shrill, jarring sound which shattered the peaceful dawn – was accompanied by the noise of hurrying footsteps down in the street, and by voices calling to each other and intermingling chaotically. Courrier, lying sleepless, heard with gratitude that something had happened which enabled him to shake off his immobility and act, abandoning his wearying marriage bed. He was ready in a flash; he snatched up his glasses and left the house. Agnès too had sat bold upright, numbed by insomnia. Now she sank back on to her pillow. For the uninitiated, a night without sleep is like torture, and leaves you feeling as drained as an invalid.

It must have been around five-thirty, on a pale morning at the end of September 1911. Lying there, with the bed finally to herself, Agnès thought with relief that, since the bell had rung here, in their village, nothing could have happened to the vet. He lived over the hill, a safe distance from the fire; he may not even have heard the echo of the bell. Her mind at rest on that score, she permitted herself a moment of Christian commiseration for whichever poor souls were suffering this misfortune. She had no clear idea of what a house fire involved. Her family used to talk about one which had happened when she was still small. That fire had started at night as well, and her father had rushed off to help, but there hadn't been much anyone could do: it was summer, so the whole place had literally gone up in smoke. This time, in the cool autumn air, there would surely be less damage: it would be a case of somebody getting a bit of a fright, that was all, and a lot of disruption.

The bell had stopped; the footsteps had died away. Through its streets, which acted like an ear trumpet, the village relayed the muffled sound of distant voices. Agnès recited a *Pater Ave Gloria*, to propitiate the heavens, and drifted gently off to sleep.

"Get up, Agnès. Put the coffee on. Now." Alphonse was standing in the bedroom doorway, and he wasn't coming in. His face was ashen and his voice was hard. He did not repeat his command, but stood there until he saw she was on her feet, then turned his back, and went down to the kitchen.

"Dear God, what can have happened?" Agnès asked herself, her heart in her mouth, as she struggled into her clothes. Perhaps someone in the crowd had said something to Alphonse, and now he was as furious as a vengeful deity. Someone they hadn't noticed the other day, when the vet –

"Dear God," she thought again, and she hurriedly recited another *Pater Ave Gloria*, for a less noble – but, she felt, more pressing – reason.

"The fire was at the carpenters'," he said, when she joined him in the kitchen.

"Ah, the Joffres'?" Agnès said, taking a deep breath. "Did the volunteers get there in time?" As she spoke, she was looking for the water and the pan used for coffee, pulling her hair back from her face.

"It must have spread easily there; with all that wood around," she went on, to disguise her husband's silence. "I suppose the whole workshop went up, did it? That's terrible, when you think of the price of wood these days." Silence fell again. Agnès busied herself at the stove, calmer now, more able to face her husband's unresponsiveness.

"We'll have to do something for those poor people, if they've lost their house." She ladled out the coffee, even though it was still too weak. Alphonse took a cup mechanically, sipped at it, then put it back down on the table, pushing it away with his fingertips. He pulled a half-smoked cigar from his pocket and lit it.

"Later on I'll visit Madame Chinot to find out more. We'll work something out for the three of them."

"Two," Alphonse corrected.

"Sorry?"

"She's dead."

"That plain woman I used to see in church? How terrible!" Agnès, horrified and curious, went to the table, and sat down opposite her husband. But he was smoking, and he said nothing more, but succumbed to a violent coughing fit that brought tears to his eyes. Agnès decided she had better visit Madame Chinot at once. Something this big called for a communal effort: the entire village had been bereaved. She waited impatiently for Alphonse to leave the table and go out to the shop, then ran upstairs to check that the children were still asleep. She combed her hair neatly, found a shawl, and went out, leaving the front door ajar.

THIRTY-FIVE

I think it is time we turned all our attention to Alphonse
Courrier: a man who, for the third time, had been duped, or
caught unawares, by life. And all this just at a time when
caution had been at his side, guiding him wisely, at least in
terms of conventional wisdom. But then, conventional wisdom
had never struck him as very satisfactory; he had always relegated it to a supporting role in his deliberations, and again
now, alone in his shop at seven-thirty in the morning, he told
himself that this was all Adèle's fault. Adèle had been the
one who had wanted to take precautions, who hadn't wanted
to expose him to the gossip of some nosy housewife. Adèle
had been the one. Adèle, who – dressed by the village women,
as best they could, in borrowed clothes – now lay inside the
dark church, because her own house was no longer there for
her to lie in.

Nobody in the village was sleeping, except perhaps the children. There is something exciting about tragedy, especially
when it doesn't affect us personally – in which case it tends to
engender a laudable industriousness. Everyone had been doing
their bit, and were trying their best to keep helping. Alphonse
could see it in the toing and froing at the church door; he
could hear it in the air, which was dripping with words of
sympathy. He was willing to bet that he wouldn't sell a nail
all day – it felt like a public holiday. Later on, he saw his wife
entering the church, in her smart clothes, to pay her respects
to a person who, when alive, it had never occurred to her to

address. And so it was with everyone. But this inconsistency could be explained: their not knowing her was precisely what compelled them, now, to verify in person that it really was she – Adèle – who had died. They needed to fix her firmly in their minds, before losing her for ever. It was a last-minute salvage operation, to ensure that they wouldn't, one day, discover they knew nothing at all about a woman who had fleetingly enjoyed such great popularity.

"Alphonse," said Agnès. "You ought to get changed and go to church to visit that poor woman." She actually said "visit". Alphonse assented meekly. Why should he escape a duty which nobody else was shirking?

"I'll stay here," she continued, "so that you won't have to shut the shop. Don't worry: I can always say you'll be back in a minute. Go right now, if you want."

Madame Courrier had come in with the two boys, who were bewildered at their mother's unusual behaviour, and full of curiosity at the prospect of staying on with her in their father's den. The ironmonger left the counter, glanced round to check everything was in its place, and went out. By now it was around nine o'clock on Saturday morning. Tomorrow would be Sunday, and there was bound to be a crush in church – a crowd that would make Christmas look like a wet Tuesday.

And, sure enough, Alphonse dressed as he would do on high days and holidays: in the black suit he had worn on his wedding day. He would have to keep shop in his smart clothes until noon. He had put on his white shirt which, he reflected, would probably get covered in dust from the counter, in spite of the long sleeves on his overalls. But, under the circumstances, Agnès wasn't going to complain about an extra shirt to wash. He left the house and made his way to the church, where he paused for a moment in front of the half-open door, to let the haberdasher and her husband come out. He returned their polite greeting, then plunged into the gloom of the nave, heading for the light of the few candles placed around the coffin.

Alphonse did not stay long in contemplation of that face, with its closed eyes. Just long enough to reflect that, in all those years, he had never once seen her sleeping.

He went straight back to the shop, where Agnès was looking anxious, constantly warning the boys not to touch anything. She greeted him with relief, and with approval for his attire.

"I'll have lunch ready at twelve today. Perhaps . . ." she added, with a hint of embarrassment, "I ought to make enough for – your friend, the doctor. He may want to come here this morning. If you see him, tell him he's welcome to join us. If you agree . . ."

Of course he agreed.

Alphonse waited until she'd gone out before he took off his jacket and put on his overalls. He fished the cigar he had extinguished an hour earlier out of the overalls pocket. He couldn't find his matches and, as he searched for them among the objects on the counter, he noticed that his hand was shaking. It was still trembling as he lifted the small flame up to his face. Then, all of a sudden, the tears began. He hadn't been expecting them: he had never cried in his life – not so far as he remembered, at any rate. He made no effort to stop. These tears were a sort of haemorrhage, through which he glimpsed a different world: a hazy, muffled world, because when one is crying, external sounds can be hard to distinguish.

THIRTY-SIX

An examination of the balance sheet of village secrets would have revealed that the Courrier family's contribution had remained constant: on the same day in which Alphonse lost a lover, his wife was discovering that she had a suitor. Not that his love was necessarily requited, but at least she was, through him, learning to recognise the outward signs of passion. Passion, after all, is not to be scorned, when offered. Agnès, far from scornful, nourished the vet's devotion skilfully: regal in the way she condescended to be loved; positively frugal when it came to physical expression of that same love. Frugal, cautious, but not entirely unwilling.

It had become customary that Alphonse, for reasons of his own, would stay on late at the shop on Tuesdays and Fridays. Such narrow windows of opportunity – especially when tried and tested by experience – can be convenient for clandestine lovers. Both Madame Courrier and her admirer knew this, although, in innocent times, neither of them had ever chosen to scrutinise this particular habit of Alphonse's. Marriages, like friendships, sometimes develop areas in which one or the other partner has no influence. All it takes is one occasion when – out of pride, or laziness – the matter is not raised, and a shadow falls over the subject. From then on, it becomes indelicate to broach it. The whole business just isn't spoken about, and this silence is the first brick in a wall which rises very slowly, but is as solid as the work of a master builder.

Alphonse's late evenings in the shop had never been the

subject of investigation, whatever his good wife may have thought about them – and, by the way, those late evenings continued.

They continued after Adèle Joffre's funeral had been conducted with affecting solemnity, in the presence of a grieving village and two weeping brothers. Nobody missed this opportunity to offer their condolences to the two men who had – for a second time – been so abruptly orphaned. The queue that formed to shake their hands was long, the offers of help plentiful. In church, it was the vet who sat between Agnès and the children: Alphonse had had to slip into the pew behind, because he had lingered outside for a minute.

It was Sunday. The new week began, still in the aftershock of the tragedy, with everybody eager to give a hand wherever necessary.

Alphonse contributed too, selecting from his stock anything that might help the Joffre brothers rebuild their house and storerooms, then going to deliver the materials in person. Until the morning of the fire, he had never been to the Joffres' house; now he felt he was being summoned back there by an indistinct feeling which he chose not to examine. He just went, unloaded his cart, and exchanged a few words with Joseph, the brother who had dragged Adèle out of her smoke-filled room. He looked very like his sister. Alphonse studied the carpenter's face as the other man thanked him with a few polite words. When Joseph asked the cost of the tools, Alphonse made a vague gesture of refusal, without uttering a syllable.

He returned to the shop and went behind the counter to wait. This was his kingdom; he felt at ease here, and he let his thoughts range freely. In those days Alphonse still worked alone.

For the first time ever, Alphonse Courrier experienced the sensation that his den was airless. And it wasn't just the shop. The whole village felt oppressive. He remembered a time just before his wedding, when he had taken a trip to Paris. To a Frenchman, Paris is the only city. Suddenly he was struck by the idea of becoming a Parisian himself – of ditching everything and going away. This vision lasted for no more than half a minute: what does an ironmonger do in the capital? He opens an ironmonger's shop. A shop stands in a street, or a square; a shop has other buildings facing it, people walking past it, four walls and a ceiling to enclose you. For an ironmonger, there is no difference whatsoever between Paris or a village. For Alphonse Courrier, who was finding it hard to breathe in his village square, a city would be no more salubrious.

His mind turned to other horizons. Then Germaine's husband came in. He needed studs for his horse's harness, which he threw down on the counter. The two men took a while to work out the measurements. Two or three more customers came in and, as they waited, the conversation drifted from one subject to another: the fire; the weather (it was starting to get cool in the evenings); the two brothers who were rebuilding their house.

"One of those boys, at least, is going to have to get married now," somebody said. "She worked like a slave for them both."

"Poor woman," came the usual refrain. "She never had a thing. Nobody would deny she was ugly; she had no fun, no friends, and no-one to pay her any compliments. She never even had a dance in her life."

"You have to admit she was unsociable, though. Did you ever see her stop for a chat, or pay any attention to anyone in the village? It's what my wife was saying yesterday, in church. Don't get me wrong, it's terrible of course, but you can't say you'd notice that she's gone –" Germaine's husband, who had voiced this last opinion, looked around in search of assent.

But it appeared he had said something unpopular – perhaps he'd said it too soon, when people's emotions were still fresh. They didn't want to give up an object of pity so quickly.

Which is why the rash speaker was left glancing uncertainly at the blank expressions which surrounded him. To make matters worse, the carter was from outside the village.

The other outsider was the vet. He wasn't in the shop that Monday morning, but sooner or later he was going to raise the subject of Adèle with Alphonse. They had spoken about her a little over lunch, on the Saturday of the fire, and then again after the funeral, when Agnès had had to improvise a simple meal, because the ceremony had dragged on, what with the burial and everything. These had been general comments, made while the shock was still resonating. But sooner or later, during some man-to-man chat, Adèle Joffre's unhappy end was going to come up.

Alphonse was finding it harder and harder to breathe.

THIRTY-SEVEN

It was a Tuesday evening towards the end of September, and it was already dark at eight o'clock. The big church doors were shut. So was the ironmonger's opposite: not a beam of light filtered out through the shutters. A weak lamp was burning in the back of the shop, and the shopkeeper was sitting behind the counter in the half-light. His customary golden glow looked somewhat tarnished; his cigar seemed to burn less brightly. He could still have been a fine Rembrandt, behind rather dusty glass.

Six hundred metres away, in the alley, the door of the Courrier house was shut. The children were asleep upstairs; in the kitchen, Agnès Courrier was sitting down peacefully, sewing. She had cleared the table, washed the dishes, and swept up the crumbs from dinner. The house was like a mirror in which she contemplated her own virtue, at the same time as keeping an eye on the fire, to make sure it didn't die down.

"It's going to be a hard winter. The dogs' coats are growing thick this year. We'll all be needing a lot of wood . . ."

"Alphonse has already stocked up. We've never had to worry about heat."

"You're right – your house is always warm. It's to do with your position as well – you're completely surrounded by other houses. The cold can't get in."

I imagine that it barely needs stating who was conversing with Agnès on that Tuesday evening, in a September already tinged with autumn. It was Alphonse Courrier's friend, the vet, "the Doctor", and now, for Madame Courrier, "François". It was probably years since anybody had called him by his first name. All he had received from her, so far, was an occasional passionate kiss, a few moments of abandonment, and – most importantly – that name. For the vet, this christening was as good as a rebirth. Now, at his sweetheart's side, he would have to experience the adolescent stage of their love and wait for it to mature. When it did, she too would feel unafraid and ready. Both of them had long outgrown the athleticism of youth, so they allowed their relationship a longer gestation period: a period which had its own charm, born of that last vestige of restraint; that reluctance to cross the boundary into a territory from which one returns completely changed, or not at all. This, at least, is what they thought – knowing nothing, or almost nothing, about such matters.

The comparatively extensive experience of Alphonse Courrier – who was now sitting alone in the half-light of the shop – could have begun to confirm their view, had he been consulted. Life had disdainfully outplayed him: that is what Courrier was thinking to himself. It had wedged him into a wretched cubby-hole from where he could see almost nothing, and had tricked him into believing the view was the widest in the world. As things stood now, however, he couldn't bring himself to be interested in seeing more. He had dismissed the idea of living in Paris . . . He had never seen the sea, but so what? He was perfectly familiar with the water in the volcanic lakes nearby, and the water in the river. The sea was just more water . . . Another woman? Another woman would not be Adèle. Such thoughts were pouring from his brain with the ease of obvious truths. It was obvious: Adèle had been his whole life.

He removed his cigar from his mouth, tapped the ash onto the floor, and spread it around with the toe of his shoe.

At about half-past nine – a late hour for a man to be the only guest in the house of a married woman – the vet, with obvious effort, rose from his kitchen chair, followed by Agnès' gaze.

"Alphonse will be at home tomorrow evening," she said. "If you'd like to come, he'd be delighted." And, in the meantime, Agnès would be savouring her secret. She was discovering the pleasure of observing from the wings, receiving coded messages consisting of waves of secret warmth. And she liked the fact that Alphonse was their unknowing witness. Tomorrow "François" would become "Doctor", and he would rise to his feet politely when the time came for her to leave them to their man-to-man chat.

THIRTY-EIGHT

Two men, alone, embody the most ancient form of human communication. Two men, whoever they may be – strangers even – rediscover an animal intimacy which dates from the beginning of time, and speak, when they choose to speak, the most ancient language in the human repertoire.

Alphonse and his friend the vet were sitting at the table in the Courriers' kitchen. Before leaving the two of them to their evening together, Agnès had raked the embers into a neat pile in the fireplace. Now she was gone, safe in the knowledge that she would not easily be forgotten. The tidily arranged embers were meant to represent her in the eyes of her admirer, who had looked on as she astutely paraded her graceful movements before him. For she had become more graceful – her husband had noticed it too, because one does not lay a gin trap for a single prey. But the iron teeth of the trap will lacerate each victim differently. For the vet they reopened a recent wound; in the case of his friend, the real woman in front of them became confused with the increasingly intrusive memory of another.

Home was beginning to feel as oppressive to Alphonse as everywhere else.

"You prefer wine to spirits, don't you?" Alphonse asked his friend. He poured generously, filling the glass right to the brim, even letting a drop overflow, without thinking of the tablecloth.

"It's going to be a hard winter, Alphonse. I'll be having

trouble with my animals from now on. Still, I don't mind – so long as there's work to do. But you should know that. You work very hard."

Alphonse lowered the glass from his lips. Was this a friendly reproach, an observation, or a compliment? We, of course, know that the vet was fishing for information. There was nothing devious about this; the older man didn't mean to insinuate anything: he just needed to know the facts, so as not to cause himself unnecessary harm. The undecipherable logic of love is very different from that of adultery. A shining illusion animates the dawn of a relationship: the belief that you are not stealing anything from anyone because a man is, after all, free to give, and if he does it generously . . . A precarious argument, however you look at it, and one which lovers seldom elaborate on because, in the long run, it becomes very hard to sustain. The mind of a man in love has room only for his private mixture of pain and joy, in which all else is forgotten. The memory will return to him later, in the form of guilt. That is when betrayal begins.

At that moment the vet would have liked his friend to see and understand the momentous change which was stirring in him. But how could a man like Alphonse comprehend such things? This was the question the elderly vet asked himself, not unreasonably. A legitimate instinct for self-preservation convinced him that the man who had possessed the object of his desire before he had, such a man could not have grasped its full worth.

"I work as hard as I have to, the same as anyone," Alphonse said, as the lamplight revealed the slight signs of ageing on his face. He returned eagerly to his glass.

"A shop is a great responsibility, my boy," the vet continued. "You've run yours perfectly all these years. You made an excellent job of building it up from nothing. You've sacrificed your time to it. Shopkeeping is the kind of thing you have to have a flair for. I have a flair for animals and you –"

" – have a flair for nails." Alphonse concluded. His voice was beginning to slur. "D'you know, Doctor, I haven't slept a wink for – for nights and nights. D'you know that?"

"Because of the shop?"

Alphonse burst out laughing. He shut his eyes for a moment. When he reopened them, they were full of tears.

"You must be joking, Doctor. Do you think a man of my age and my character would lose sleep over a shop? I thought you knew me – surely you know I wouldn't let a shop keep me awake."

"Alphonse, are you ill? If you are, for God's sake go and see a doctor. Don't hang about. Remember you've got the children to think about."

"And a wife. A wife I swore in church to support 'till death do us part'. Death do us part –"

"Well, why don't you go then?"

"Because I'm perfectly healthy. It's just that I'm not sleeping. There's no reason to sleep."

"There's a physiological reason, my friend. You can't escape that, any more than anyone else can. If you don't sleep for a while you start to lose strength. You can't think straight. You didn't even notice you weren't making sense just now: 'There's no reason to sleep.' Is that a rational thing to say? What's up, Alphonse?"

The question was an inadvertently fearful one, with two threads running through it: the old friendship between the two men and the vet's new passion. Courrier devoted his attention to his glass again, then looked up at his friend with eyes which were tired, but whose pupils were dazzlingly blue. It looked like the effects of fever, or God knows what other devilry.

"I think it might be old age," Alphonse said. "Doesn't it happen to you? They say you sleep less as you get older."

"You're forty-four, Alphonse. That's not old. And you slept well enough until a little while ago – didn't you?"

"A little while ago – It's that little while that's made the difference. You don't become old overnight. There's a point when you begin to age. I think I must have started becoming one of you – I'm sorry, that was a stupid thing to say. But I've said it now." Alphonse's voice sounded all wrong, almost like a drunk's. The vet had stiffened for a moment, long enough to reflect that you're as old as you feel; he'd never felt as young as he did now. His friend was obviously troubled by something which sooner or later he would confide.

"Perhaps. If so, welcome to the club!" he said, seeking to defuse Alphonse's comment. There was something in Alphonse which was moving him deeply. So deeply that he reached out to pat his hand reassuringly. They had a long winter ahead in which to talk, and at that moment the vet was thinking that he would divide his life equally between love and friendship, under this one roof. He could see nothing contradictory in this plan, even the fact that his friend was the husband of the woman he loved.

"Do you know what it means to feel sorrow for someone?"

Alphonse's question was unclear, and the vet found it disconcerting.

"Naturally," he answered. "We all do. As you so rightly pointed out, I am not so young that I haven't been through – but what are you driving at?"

Because Alphonse was clearly driving at something, and the vet felt his suspicions suddenly aroused. Sorrow for someone: what kind of sorrow? For whom? For his wife, who no longer – ? "Dear God," Agnès had murmured, the first time he kissed her.

"What sorrow, Alphonse?"

The unfortunate man believed the moment of reckoning was nigh and, if so, the sooner it arrived the better.

"In my life, I've had cause to be grateful to two women: the one who brought me into the world, and the one who opened herself to me that first time. I've lost them both."

"What?" the doctor asked. What did he mean, "both"? Alphonse's mother had died years before, and he had taken the loss very well. So? What did he mean by this? He must be speaking – in veiled terms – of his wife. The vet's life was most definitely not going to be divided equally between love and friendship; the vet's life was collapsing all around him. There was nothing to be done.

"Listen, Alphonse –" began the vet, like the honest man he was.

"No, no, please. I'm just rambling," Alphonse interrupted. "Don't worry. Everything passes. Lying awake these last few nights I've been thinking I ought to go away. I feel stifled even here, as I'm talking to you. I've been left with this obsession that now I'm the one who's being asphyxiated."

"Who have you lost, Alphonse?"

Gradually, as if a curtain of smoke were lifting and clearing the view ahead of him, the vet was confronted with a disconcerting landscape.

Alphonse did not reply.

THIRTY-NINE

Sharing another man's pain is an act of generosity, and to be generous you have to be free – free, in the first instance, from pain of your own. Let us consider the case of Courrier and his friend, on an evening at the end of September 1911, when one of the two was being tormented by a desolation more terrible than any he had ever felt before. His companion – suddenly unburdened of his fear – was watching, without averting his eyes for an instant from the wound which, a moment before, he hadn't even known existed. All selfishness forgotten, all concern for himself evaporated, the vet felt nothing but bewildered compassion for his friend. He could understand Alphonse perfectly, because he who, in similar circumstances (Heaven forfend), would have experienced the same agony, was not experiencing it now. He was not having to feel grief himself, so hearing it in his friend's broken voice stirred within him an emotion which was both powerful and cheap. It was like watching a play.

"I could never have imagined that you . . . But what about your wife?"

This question had the effect of bringing the vet back to himself. In his mind he had separated Madame Courrier from Agnès, but now the two abruptly coalesced, and the image of the woman he venerated rose in front of him, betrayed. Before he'd had time to consider the usefulness of such a precedent in unburdening his own conscience and that of his new lover, he was overcome with indignation. But indignation was soon tempered by the compassion of love, now that he too knew what love was, and could empathise. Indignant and understanding: he could be both at once.

Alphonse had far too much on his mind to notice the sudden changes in his friend's expression.

"I made sure my wife never lacked for anything – children included," he said. "I never gave her any grounds for suspicion. I never caused her any pain. She's been happy – she is happy – with her life. She's got a respectable home and she's got two sons who take after her; two sons who are nothing like me. I take care of practicalities and let her be mistress in here, as I am master in my shop. And what a master I have been!" He lifted his head, like an exiled monarch who still feels the ghost of a crown upon his head.

The vet passed a hand over his eyes, because, for one moment, Alphonse's crown looked more grotesque than noble.

"Everything changes, my friend," said the older man, articulating his vision. Everything changes: the monarch was now a wreck, while the betrayed woman was being reborn through another man's desire.

"In any case, doctor, I can truly say that I have been happy." How many people could state that unequivocally? Even in the midst of his own turbulent passion, the vet could not conceal from himself his reverent envy. He had always believed Alphonse to be happy, but he'd imagined his happiness to be a colder emotion. Now he was discovering that Alphonse was already intimately acquainted with that country which he himself was still viewing tentatively from the border.

"I'm so sorry, Alphonse. I can imagine what you must be feeling. You hid it very well – the whole thing, I mean."

"We were lucky, for years. Or maybe, in some way or other, all this was meant to be. Otherwise we'd have been found out."

The vet was listening attentively: in the old days they'd have called her death the judgment of God.

"And what now?" he asked. "What are you going to do?" Alphonse's story was coinciding dangerously with his own. The vet's old friend might become an unwitting hindrance – which is why the doctor posed this question with greatly increased emotion and trepidation.

"I'll do what I've always done," Alphonse replied. "I'm not going to change my routine in the slightest. It's the only way I can protect Adèle's memory, in case someone – but no, that would never happen. Nobody – except you, now, and I trust you implicitly – would ever suspect a thing. You all thought she was too ugly to be – loved." Alphonse began to laugh, so that the tears which had been gathering in his eyes began to fall, and looked like tears of mirth. "I'll go on shutting myself away in the shop till late on Tuesdays and Fridays, as I've always done. Alone. I'll be alone now, and I'm sure I'll find things to do. You all thought I was up to my eyes in work – I won't be short of it now. If I look into it, I'll probably find that I'm behind."

"You know what I'm thinking?" he asked, narrowing his eyes and looking sidelong at the vet. "I'll extend the shop; enlarge the business. From now on I'm going to be rich. Where I used to earn a hundred francs, I'll earn three hundred. My sons will never have to worry about money – " He lit his cigar, drew on it deeply, coughed, and turned it round to contemplate its glowing end.

"I'm forty-four. By the age of fifty I will have arrived. Do you know what I mean by 'arrived'? I mean I'll have reached the shore: I'll have reached dry land, my friend."

The vet, listening in amazement, let him ramble on. Perhaps Alphonse's mind had become intoxicated with wild dreams of money to assuage a pain he could not otherwise contain.

But the shopkeeper's eyes were animated and sparkling blue; his voice clear and confident.

"How swiftly human passion fades!" the older man thought bitterly to himself. One barely had time to witness a soul's last agony, before it was rising from its own ashes, pushing the spectator aside: from tragedy to vaudeville in a single evening.

The two men parted company. Each returned to his own torment; Alphonse's was no less agonising for his recent burst of enthusiasm, which had appeared to herald such changes in his life. He climbed the stairs slowly, undressed in the dark so as not to wake his wife, and sank onto the bed, pulling the covers up to his chin. Sleep was not going to come.

The other man went over the hill on his cart, very slowly, and was swallowed up by the night.

FORTY

From 1911 to the end of 1917, nothing of obvious significance occurred. A war broke out, but it brought no great changes to the Courrier household. The boys were too young, and Alphonse too old, for conscription. The war did not even affect them financially: if anything, as is often the case, it seemed to be facilitating that bid for wealth which, one September evening, in the ears of the bewildered vet, had sounded almost blasphemous.

At times, the elderly doctor's thoughts still turned to Alphonse's story.

"No man who has truly loved could hurtle so single-mindedly towards wealth," he would think to himself, "or lift his head again so soon after a blow of that kind. If Agnès died I – I would die too." Such were the vet's innermost feelings, and he would find himself repeatedly banishing, then calling back, this tragic image, as an affirmation of his love. Alphonse had always been a cold, confident sort of man. Of course, now, he missed that poor woman who had suffocated so tragically in her own bed – missed her physically. It was at this point that the vet would realize, with a shudder, that Courrier could, should he so desire, satisfy such a physical need with his lawfully wedded wife.

In truth, something inside Alphonse had snapped like a broken bone, which ligaments and muscles still struggle in vain to hold together.

He threw himself into his work. His eyes darkened; his cigar glowed vigorously. His hands were restless. The two evenings a week he had previously devoted to love were no longer enough: money demanded more time, and more energy. He had six years in which to reach his port of destination. Since Fate, in his opinion, had wrongfooted him too often already, he felt that the time had come to take firm control.

Life became a well-oiled machine: his work; his home; the friends he saw at the inn, two evenings a week, to discuss the ways of the world; and his old confidant, the vet, who clearly preferred the evenings he spent at Courrier's house, in a simulation of family life – which was understandable, since he had no-one. The elderly man fondly devoted himself to the two boys, caring for them and watching them grow; commending their mother's strictness and shaking his head over their little failings. He had taken them in hand. There was a sense in which Alphonse's confession had orphaned them in the doctor's mind.

It was the vet who took them to the city for the first time. They went to Clermont-Ferrand, accompanied by Agnès, who wore her travelling outfit and sat, very straight-backed, on the cart, which was beginning to look distinctly old-fashioned. Several motor-cars overtook them along the way.

"Alphonse will buy one of those sooner or later," commented François, and the boys laughed excitedly. Why else make so much money?

The shop had deepened, in a manner of speaking: the cellar had been turned into a well-stocked storeroom. The old shelves had been moved downstairs, and the ground floor modernised. There were two assistants who worked there on and off, until they were taken on full-time, to make up for the owner's frequent absences: Alphonse always went to choose his stock in person.

The villagers looked on, largely unsurprised, as Alphonse's wealth grew. His quest for riches had not changed him a bit:

he was as polite as ever, and never showed undue attachment to the money which passed through his hands in such quantity. The idea of being rich didn't really interest him: money was no more than an instrument he needed to carry out a project. His attitude, had it been known, would have seemed strange in a society which had already made money its goal – so strange, that it occurred to nobody. Not even to Agnès. She appreciated the comforts her husband procured for her, and enjoyed the sight of her two sons growing up strong and healthy. Her conscience was almost completely clear. It was true that once, years before, she had briefly yielded to a passion, but that passion had belonged to somebody else – all she could ever do was witness it, unable to feel anything more than the distant glow of its searing heat. She had allowed herself to be loved by the man who, now, was always at her side, like a protective deity, but the capacity to love simply wasn't in her. Love is something you have to be cut out for, so to speak; Agnès, when it came down to it, found love unseemly and embarrassing.

Theirs was a relationship some aspects of which had been shelved, while others had been converted into faithfulness and melancholy.

The villagers had no idea that they had been in such proximity to two sensational cases of adultery. Village life had proceeded along a well-laid path, with few surprises. People clearly remembered the time Germaine wore a red dress to a christening, and the fire at the Joffre's house, but Adèle's face was nothing more than a confused memory. A few of them even forgot the date of the tragedy.

In 1916 the ironmonger's shop ended the year comfortably in the black. Profits had been reinvested: some went into a fund for the running of the shop; some to the prudently evaluated purchase of land to the south of the village, where the farming was always good, and the rest to buy two houses in the centre of Clermont-Ferrand. Soon after his birthday, and the celebrations for the dawn of 1917 (which was given a warm welcome, despite being the third year of the war), Courrier was invited to move into politics. His property in Clermont made him eligible for a career in the département. He refused without ceremony or hesitation. His only regret was the disappointed look in the eyes of the two men delivering the invitation. He'd never liked letting people down. Agnès felt the disappointment even more keenly, but kept it to herself: her husband had already given her a great deal; that much was undeniable.

Winter ended with a late, and heavy, snowfall. Summer burst forth unexpectedly, far in advance of the calendar. Everybody complained, with the exception of Alphonse, who looked on from the cool of his shop like a man watching a show from his theatre box. From time to time he would stand in his doorway and gaze out at the massive church, the scorching square, and the slow steps of the few people who could not avoid walking across the baking cobble-stones. Then he would step back inside and – in the quiet intervals between customers – count his takings methodically, calculating and comparing them with those of previous months and years.

A short while before Christmas he did his annual accounts, and assessed the results in the light of those six years of relentless work. Everything was perfect; the figures all balanced exactly. Not even in Clermont-Ferrand could a shop have done better. At the thought of this, he felt a wave of pride and nostalgia.

He initialled the ledger, dated it the 23rd of December 1917, closed it, and went home.

FORTY-ONE

They found him on the morning of the 27th of December. The snow had let up briefly. They found him in his shop. One side of his jaw had been shattered by a clumsy pistol-shot. Higher up, there was a clean hole in his temple. There was not a great deal of blood; the place was tidy. The pistol lay at his side, while, on the floor, his other hand had let slip a spent cigar.

This last object was picked up by the vet: the first person to come into the shop, through the back door, and the first to witness this strange scene. Even Alphonse's glasses were still intact. The whole thing made sense to the old horse-doctor; it was crystal clear. The only detail which was to torment him, stubbornly lodged in his memory, was the shriek let out by Agnès Duval, as she stood silhouetted in the back doorway. He had no power to stop her.

With the echo of that dreadful cry the Courrier affair detonated instantly, like a grenade in a field, and its mysterious resonance lingered long in the memory of the inhabitants of the village of Orcival, in the Auvergne.